"I figured I should spend the night."

Joe's tone was entirely professional but, as he stood in her doorway, Rowena was deeply aware of his eyes on her. She felt self-conscious, yet strangely exhilarated. "You saw him?"

He nodded. "Yeah, that thug has been lurking around your house again."

"I know. But he didn't do anything threatening. I don't think he'll be back tonight."

Joe didn't seem convinced. "So you want me to leave?"

"No!" The word was out before she could stop it. She spun around out of the doorway, heard him come inside and shut the door behind him. "There's a bedroom on the second floor you can use, unless you want to remain on the first floor to watch for bogeymen."

"Rowena," he said.

"What?" Slowly she turned around.

He looked at her intensely. "If I'm going to protect you, I'll need to be a lot closer to you than that."

Dear Reader,

What is more appealing, more enduring than *Cinderella, Beauty and the Beast* and *Pygmalion*? Fairy tales and legends are basic human stories, retold in every age, in their own way. Romance stories, at their heart, are the happily ever after of every story we listened to as children. That was the inspiration for our 1993 yearlong Lovers & Legends miniseries. Each month, one book is a fairy tale retold in sizzling Temptation-style!

This month's Lovers & Legends book is based on the popular tale of *Rapunzel.* The heroine of *Night Watch,* Rowena Willow, is a beautiful, brilliant woman living a private, withdrawn existence...until Joe Scarlatti enters her life. Startlingly sexy Joe teaches her to let down her hair and become the exciting woman she's always wanted to be.

In the coming months we have stories from bestselling authors Tiffany White, *Naughty Talk* (*Legend of Sir Gawain*) and Kristine Rolofson, *I'll Be Seeing You* (*Christmas Legend*).

We hope you enjoy the rest of our magical Lovers & Legends miniseries and all the other fantastic Temptation novels coming out in 1993. All we can say about 1994's lineup of Temptation books is...look out! To celebrate our tenth anniversary, we'll be publishing books chock-full of passion, humor, adventure...and so unpredictable, they're sure to give you a thrill!

Birgit Davis-Todd
Senior Editor

P.S. We love to hear from our readers.

Night Watch
Carla Neggers

Harlequin Books

TORONTO • NEW YORK • LONDON
AMSTERDAM • PARIS • SYDNEY • HAMBURG
STOCKHOLM • ATHENS • TOKYO • MILAN
MADRID • WARSAW • BUDAPEST • AUCKLAND

Published October 1993

ISBN 0-373-25561-6

NIGHT WATCH

Prologue

JOE SCARLATTI had a book and a beer and figured to ride out the fourth straight day of San Francisco fog in his booth at Mario's Bar & Grill.

His cousin ran the waterfront place. Joe had a couple of rooms upstairs. It hadn't always been that way, but it was that way now. And it wasn't a bad life. After close to six months, Joe had almost gotten to the point where he enjoyed it.

Almost.

He spotted Hank Ryan making his way through the swirling, milky fog outside the window and put down his book. Hank was a fellow cop. A *working* cop. He believed Joe should be working, too. He stopped by about once a week to tell him so.

Joe felt the dampness of the fog when Hank opened the door. It was midafternoon and the place was quiet, just Joe with his book, a few stragglers, Mario clanking around in the kitchen.

The tourists and cheap-eats types had yet to discover Mario's Bar & Grill. It was not a fancy place. Booths, a long bar of dark, aged oak, a worn hardwood floor, a jukebox and a couple of video games in back—that was it. Mario's had been known for good food and fair prices since Joe and his cousin's grandfather—Mario, Sr.—had started the place the week after Prohibition ended.

Hank plopped into the booth across from Joe, uninvited. Hank was a big man. Bigger than Joe, African-American, smart. Cops didn't come any smarter than Hank Ryan. He knew the law, but more than that he knew people. He was a sergeant with the potential of being a captain.

Joe was a sergeant, too. Technically.

"*Moby Dick?*" Hank shook his head. "You are in bad shape, Scarlatti."

"It's 'a damp, drizzly November in my soul,'" Joe quoted dryly. "Now I know what Ishmael meant when he said that. Something wrong with reading?"

"No, but *Moby Dick?* Why the hell don't you read something fun?"

"*Moby Dick* is fun."

Hank shook his head again, regarding Joe with the mix of despair and disgust he usually reserved for repeat offenders.

"You want something to drink?" Joe asked, knowing Hank stayed away from alcohol.

"No. You look like hell, Joe. I'm surprised Mario hasn't thrown you out."

"He does periodically, but he always lets me back in. I'm family and I pay my rent on time. And I don't look *that* bad, Hank. You're just jerking my chain."

Hank sighed. "That's why your family and friends are always on your case—so you won't burn out totally. There's no escaping us, Scarlatti. But I know there's no talking to you when you're in this mood.

Look, I've got some news I thought might interest you—Eliot Tyhurst is out of prison."

Immediately Joe felt a twist of pain and anger deep within him. "He wasn't in long enough."

"I know it. Woman who put him there is still in San Francisco. Rowena Willow." Hank pulled a crumpled scrap of paper from a pocket and shoved it across the scarred wooden table. "That's her address."

Joe looked at the scrawled name of the Telegraph Hill street, and right away he knew what Hank wanted. But he said, "What the hell kind of name is Rowena Willow, anyway? You ever wonder that?"

"Frankly, no."

"Bet she made it up. Probably born a 'Debbie' and figured it was too ordinary and changed it."

"It's for real."

"Who'd do that to a kid?"

Hank shrugged. "Her parents were kind of eccentric."

"Kind of?"

"They're dead now. Died when Rowena was eight. She moved in with an aunt even weirder than the parents. The aunt died right before Rowena nabbed Tyhurst. Now she lives alone in the aunt's house. I hear it's quite a place. I've been by it but not inside. It's right out of *Ivanhoe*. A regular castle. I'm surprised it doesn't have a moat. You've probably seen it."

"Maybe," Joe said. "I don't make a point of checking out architectural wonders. How do you know all this stuff about this Rowena character?"

"There was a lot of gossip about her during Tyhurst's trial, and I've kept track of her since, on and off. No big deal."

Hank was silent a moment. Then he said, "Tyhurst will come after her, Joe. You know he will."

"It's not my problem." The words were automatic, born less of conviction than of necessity. Nearly six months on voluntary leave hadn't convinced Joe that he belonged back on active duty. He still didn't trust himself. He pushed his empty beer bottle—only his first of the day—to one side and opened *Moby Dick*. "Count me out."

Hank didn't react. He looked around the dark, atmospheric bar. Joe Scarlatti's home. Hell of a life.

"What am I supposed to do?" Hank asked.

"What do you mean? Tyhurst has served his time. Nothing you can do."

"I've got a feeling about this one."

"Hank, the bastard's never made any threats against her that we know about. We've got no cause, can't order a watch on her."

Hank leaned forward, his gaze hard and knowing. "I was in the courtroom when the jury brought in the verdict. Rowena Willow was sitting in the same row as me. Tyhurst's eyes never left her, even when the foreman read the verdict. I've never seen such cold eyes."

Joe flipped a page in *Moby Dick*, but he wasn't reading.

"He's not going to forgive and forget, Joe. He's not the type. He's going to make Rowena Willow pay."

"No guilt trips," Joe reminded him. When he'd gone on leave, Hank had promised he wouldn't stoop to guilt trips to get Joe back on the job.

"This isn't a guilt trip, Joe. You're Rowena Willow's last chance. Maybe her only chance."

"According to your gut."

"Yeah."

Joe blew out a breath and drummed the bar with his forefinger, and Hank let him think. Mario had emerged from the kitchen and was polishing the mirror their grandfather had installed behind the bar. People, old grandpa said, should have a good look at themselves when drinking. Maybe that was why Joe had taken a booth. He didn't want to look at himself. He hadn't shaved in a couple of days, combed his hair, bothered with anything dressier than jeans and polo shirts. He knew there were dark circles under his red-streaked eyes. But for his endless walks, filling up the hours when his cousin ran him out, he would have gone to flab by now. Six months. It seemed like an eternity. He had taken a leave of absence only because he had promised his grandmother he wouldn't just up and quit. Sofia Scarlatti had suffered enough.

She and her late husband—the founder of Mario's Bar & Grill—had been among Eliot Tyhurst's victims.

Something Hank Ryan knew all too well.

"If this Rowena Willow lives on Telegraph Hill," Joe said, "she can afford to hire her own damned bodyguard."

"Yeah, but she won't. Doesn't think like that. Even if I encouraged her to hire someone, she'd just tell me I was overreacting. She lives alone, works alone, seldom if ever goes out. Hates distractions of any kind. Rowena Willow likes to keep to herself, Joe. She assumes people won't bother her if she doesn't bother them."

"Even a man she put in prison?"

"Yeah."

Hank would know. He had answered Rowena Willow's call when she'd announced to the police she had captured a bank robber. She hadn't mentioned that "captured" to her had meant that, with the help of her computer, she'd nailed him to the wall. Hank had called in the feds and the white-collar criminal guys, but he'd kept track of the case.

An ordinary bank robber—the kind he and Joe dealt with—would have done a couple of decades' time for stealing not one percent of what Eliot Tyhurst had stolen. But Tyhurst was a unique case. Once a prominent San Francisco banker, he hadn't used a gun to get what he wanted. Instead, he had used the trust people had put in him.

"He'll come after her," Hank repeated, without drama. "I saw it in his eyes three years ago. One way or another, Eliot Tyhurst is going to make Rowena Willow pay for finding him out. You know it, Joe, and I know it."

"But she doesn't."

"She doesn't think that way."

Just what way did Rowena Willow think? Joe remembered reading about the brilliant financial analyst who had unraveled Tyhurst's nefarious schemes on her own time, apparently for her own amusement. He tried to picture her and found he couldn't. "I haven't met her, have I?"

"You'd remember if you had."

Joe assumed it was because he had a good memory for faces.

"I doubt she's even aware Tyhurst is getting out," Hank added.

Joe sighed. It didn't sound good. "What is she, some kind of dingbat?"

"An eccentric genius."

"Hell. Sounds peachy. You going to talk to her?"

"Nope. I think it's best we keep our plans to ourselves."

"Hank, there is no 'we.' I haven't agreed to take this case."

"It shouldn't be tough work, you know. All you have to do is keep an eye on her place, make sure Tyhurst doesn't contact her. She doesn't even have to know you're there."

It still didn't sound good.

"Rowena Willow ruined Tyhurst, Joe. His reputation, his career. Cost him millions in fines and fees, a few years in prison."

"It wasn't enough," Joe repeated.

"No," Hank conceded. He settled back against the tall wooden booth. "Catch Tyhurst coming after Rowena Willow to exact a little revenge and we can put him away for the good, long stretch he deserves."

"Why me?"

Hank looked him straight in the eye. "You need to work, Joe."

Without responding, Joe snatched up the crumpled scrap of paper bearing Rowena Willow's name and address and slid out of the booth. He didn't look back. He walked straight to the door and into the San Francisco fog, letting it envelop him, his soul.

Behind him Hank called Mario for a cola, asked him how he was doing. He would know that Joe needed to be alone right now, just as he had known that six months was a hell of a long time for a cop to be off the streets. Just as he'd known that Joe needed to work.

Maybe this job would save him from the abyss of regret and despair he'd fallen into. Then again, maybe nothing could. Maybe it was too damned late.

1

BLEARY-EYED from a marathon session at her computer, Rowena Willow found herself stumbling into walls on the way down from her third-floor office to the kitchen. It was an enormous, drafty room with modern appliances that had been installed during her Great-Aunt Adelaide's reluctant remodeling twenty years ago, right after Rowena had come to live with her. She remembered her aunt tearfully selling a painting from an upstairs bedroom to pay for the job. Aunt Adelaide had never had any real money of her own. Rowena had vowed never to repeat the sweet but rather eccentric old woman's fate.

Or her parents' fate, she thought. But before she could probe the thought further, she dismissed it, willed it back to the far recesses of her mind. She didn't like to think too much about her parents' fate.

She put on the kettle for tea and fed her two cats, Mega and Byte. For her, romantic names. Then she did some stretches and her hand exercises, trying to work out the increasingly worrisome tingling and numbness in her fingers. She couldn't come down with carpal tunnel syndrome or any of the other repetitive-motion disorders associated with keyboard use. How would she work? What would she do with herself if she had to stay off her computer?

The kettle whistled, and she poured a little of the boiling water into her simple white porcelain two-cup pot, swirled it around to warm the pot, then dumped it into the sink. She added two heaping spoonfuls of loose-leaf English breakfast tea and filled the pot to the brim, setting it on a teak serving tray. While the brew steeped, she chose a china cup and saucer from her collection in a glass-fronted cupboard—the forget-me-not pattern, she decided. She filled a tiny white pitcher with a dollop of milk, got out the tea strainer and placed one fat honey-butter cookie on a delicate, pale blue paper napkin. Perhaps Aunt Adelaide hadn't known how to make a living, but she did teach Rowena how to do a wonderful tea.

Already feeling better, Rowena carried the tray up to her tower sunroom, not far from her office on the third floor. It jutted out from the main body of the house and had floor-to-ceiling windows on three sides with spectacular views of San Francisco. The sunwashed city glistened below her. Sailboats dotted the bay, so blue under the cloudless sky. Or maybe everything seemed brighter and clearer after the days and days of fog. Rowena opened the windows and let in the breeze, half tempted to take her tea into the courtyard behind the house.

But in the courtyard, she wouldn't have a view of the street.

After Aunt Adelaide's death, Rowena had removed from the sunroom the clunky Victorian furniture her aunt favored, replacing it with dozens of pillows of every imaginable size and shape. She could plop down wherever she wanted to on the thick Persian carpet and look out at the world, a relief at the end of a long, harrowing day working at her computer and dealing with clients. Sometimes it seemed more fun, more of a fantasy, safer, just to look out at the world rather than to go out into it.

Today she leaned back against a giant, overstuffed, tapestry pillow and set her tea tray on the floor at her side. She stretched out her legs in front of her, not on pillows, as generally would have been the case, but on the thick Persian carpet. She wanted nothing—not even her toes—to obstruct her view.

Her view not of the skyline or San Francisco Bay, but of her street.

She poured her tea through the strainer set carefully over her cup. As she set the pot down, her eyes scanned the cars crammed into coveted spaces up and down her steep, quiet, expensive street.

What kind of car would he be driving today? Yesterday it had been a modest two-door black sedan. The day before a red German sports car. The day before that a tan minivan.

She added a few drops of milk to her tea. Three days in a row he had been out there, on her street, in front of her home.

He parked in different spaces and drove different cars. Sometimes he read the newspaper and sometimes a book. Most of the time, however, he seemed just to sit there doing nothing. She didn't know if he stayed there all day; she had to work. But he was *always* there at teatime. Rowena meant to check the street first thing in the morning but she kept forgetting. With the three-hour time difference between San Francisco and Wall

Street, she liked to get an early start. And once on her computer, she concentrated only on the job at hand. Her work demanded her full attention and received it without quarrel. She had no intention of ending up like Aunt Adelaide, selling off paintings to survive.

And of course she wouldn't end up like her parents. They had been a disastrous match, feeding each other's worst instincts. Yes, they'd been happy, but they'd died young and broke.

Willing them to the back of her mind once more, Rowena set her cup back on its saucer and did a few neck rolls to ease out the stiffness, her eyes still narrowed on the street. Her hair—the color of spun gold, friends had told her—was piled up on her head, expertly pinned, not one strand errant. She wondered if its weight contributed to the stiffness in her neck. She couldn't recall when she'd last had her hair cut. It was quite long, at least to her waist, thick and naturally wavy—not that she ever wore it down. She always pinned up her hair first thing in the morning, even before brushing her teeth or checking her computer, which she kept on at all times. It was one of the ways she exacted control over her life.

Maybe he's finished what he came to do, she thought. *Maybe he's never coming back*.

She was surprised at the rush of disappointment she felt, but she didn't have a chance to examine its source.

She spotted him.

He was settled behind the wheel of a rusting, dented gray pickup truck directly beneath her window. Rolling up onto her knees, Rowena peered down through the center window, suddenly irritated by its dozens of tiny panes. She wished he would step out of the truck so she could get a good look at him. Her powers of observation and her prodigious memory were her greatest weapon. She would remember if she had seen him before. Perhaps she would be able to make an educated guess as to whether he was a thug, an undercover cop on a stakeout or a private investigator. She had already dismissed a whole host of other possibilities, including a drug dealer. A drug dealer, she reasoned, wouldn't eat powdered doughnuts in such a disreputable-looking truck; he would stick to the German sports car.

If she could see him, she knew she would be certain.

Who, she wondered, was he watching? She considered her various neighbors on the street, so many of whom she had never met, although she had lived there since she was eight years old. Any likely suspects? She supposed he could be waiting for something scheduled to happen *on* her street, but not involving anyone who actually lived there. She couldn't deny her interest: She seldom got to unravel a mystery that involved human beings rather than numbers.

The truck door opened.

Rowena held her breath, waiting.

He climbed out.

A cop. *Definitely* a cop. There was no doubt in her mind.

Nothing specific eliminated his being a thug or a private investigator. Nothing specific, even, blared police. But Rowena knew. She just knew.

Down on the street, his back to her, he stretched his arms above his head, then turned and drummed his fingers on the roof of his truck. He looked impatient and irritable. He was, Rowena saw, a thickly built man with very dark—almost black—hair and a face that was more striking than handsome, the nose crooked, the mouth rather severe. She expected that up close she would see scars. Suddenly she wanted to see him smile. What would he look like if he smiled? Would she change her mind about him? Would he have bad teeth, look goofy, menacing, dishonest?

No, she thought. A smile wouldn't erase the gravity and the stubborn sadness that seemed to cling to him.

From her position, she could see the gray sweatshirt that was stretched across his broad chest. A pair of jeans went with it. Close-fitting jeans. He would, she imagined, have muscular legs, particularly his thighs. His was a sprinter's build; he would use speed and power in a physical encounter. Any kind of physical encounter.

Heat rushed to her cheeks at the unexpected, unruly thought.

What was she thinking?

He took a deep breath, pounded the truck roof with the flat of his hand and climbed back in the driver's seat as if he'd had enough for one day. Three floors up, Rowena heard the engine race and watched him drive away.

She finished her tea, in no particular hurry.

Then she looked up the main number for the San Francisco police department. She used her cordless telephone and took it into the sunroom, where she stood in front of the windows above the now-empty parking space and made the call. She identified herself to the woman who answered and said she would like to speak to the person in charge of the undercover officer staked out on her Telegraph Hill street. She gave the name of her street and the number of her house and spelled her name. She was put on hold. In another minute a man picked up. She repeated what she wanted. He said, "You've got to be kidding," and put her on hold, and in a moment another man picked up.

"Good afternoon," she said, "my name is Rowena Willow and I—"

"I know who you are, Ms. Willow. I'm Sergeant Ryan. Hank Ryan. What's up?"

She recognized the name at once. He was the policeman who had investigated her report on Eliot Tyhurst. He had come to her house to make sure she wasn't some kind of lunatic; she wasn't sure that he hadn't decided she wasn't. But he *had* taken her findings to higher authorities. Ultimately Tyhurst had been arrested and convicted.

She wondered if she'd been handed off to him just because she was a known eccentric and he'd dealt with her before.

The thought made her angry, if not defensive. She had almost grown accustomed to people's stereotypes of her.

"Well," she said coolly, "I've spotted your man on Telegraph Hill—"

"Excuse me?"

"Your man. I spotted him. I was afraid since I spotted him, someone else might have as well. I'm particularly concerned that the subject he's watching might have seen him. I wouldn't want anything untoward to happen simply because those of you in authority didn't realize your man isn't very...subtle."

"I see."

There was a note of caution in his tone. She bit the corner of her mouth, hoping she didn't sound weird; sometimes she just didn't know. "I don't mean to be insulting."

Hank Ryan cleared his throat. "You're saying that since you made our man, some bad guy he's after might have made him, too."

"That's correct."

"What makes you think he's a cop?"

"Oh, that's obvious."

She thought she heard Ryan chuckle. She remembered him as a competent, rigorous individual who had made no derogatory remarks about her, her life-style or her work. He said, "Thanks for the tip."

Rowena bristled at being dismissed. "Check him out. He's approximately five feet ten inches tall, thickly built. He has near-black hair cut in no particular style. He doesn't shave every day. I would say his nose has been broken once or twice. My guess is a Mediterranean ethnic background, probably Italian."

Hank Ryan was silent.

"He has driven four different vehicles." She described them in detail and recited their license plate numbers which, she explained, she had memorized. "I'm observant but not suspicious by nature. Someone up to something illegal is likely to be both observant *and* suspicious and...well, I'm sure you don't want your officer stumbling into a situation in which he's dangerously over his head."

"I'm afraid he already has," the sergeant grumbled under his breath. "I'll see who we've got out there and warn him. Thanks."

She hung up wondering if she would ever see the dark-haired man again.

ROWENA WILLOW had one hell of a boring life, so far as Joe could see. Four days now and the only glimpse he'd had of her was in that damned tower room above the street. He had to crane his neck, so it was never much of a glimpse. She showed up every afternoon promptly at five-ten. What she did there he had no idea. Water plants? But he couldn't make out any plants.

He sat at Mario's bar, waiting for hot pastrami on rye. He already had his beer. Ah, reality.

Mario, a balding, good-humored man ten years Joe's senior, shoved the sandwich in front of him. "Working, Joe?"

"Doing a favor for a friend, keeping an eye out on a crazy woman." He decided not to tell him it was Rowena Willow, the financial genius who had put Eliot Tyhurst in jail.

"Pretty?"

"Doubtful. I haven't seen her yet, though."

"How can you keep an eye on her if you haven't seen her?"

Joe shook his head. "She doesn't lead a normal life, that's how. She's weird, Mario. Weird, weird, weird. So far as I can tell, she never leaves her house."

"Where's she live?"

"Telegraph Hill."

Mario paused to greet a regular customer and slide him a beer, not waiting for his order. "Fancy neighborhood."

"Yeah. It's quite a place. She has her groceries delivered, works there, doesn't seem to have any friends—and this house, Mario. Put a full moon in the background and we're talking bats and vampires. She probably has her own torture chamber."

His cousin laughed. "Maybe after this job, police work will look good again."

Joe wondered if it would.

In the mirror across from him, he saw Hank Ryan walk grim-faced into the bar. Without a word he sat down on the stool next to Joe. Mario poured him a ginger ale and Hank took a sip. Then he looked at Joe. "She made you the first day."

At first Joe didn't know what he was talking about. "Who?"

"Rowena Willow. She spotted you, Joe."

"The hell she did!"

Hank nodded. "The hell she did." He nibbled on a pretzel and repeated his bizarre telephone conversation.

Down the bar, Mario was laughing with a customer, demanding to see the I.D. of another, acknowledging the designated driver of another group—all, it seemed, at the same time. Or maybe, Joe thought, his brain was jumbled from his strange assignment. He didn't want to think about crazy ladies who lived in strange houses.

In his twelve years as a cop, five working undercover, Joe Scarlatti had never—not once—been made.

He glanced sideways at Hank, who looked tired, still in his uniform. Joe hadn't asked about Hank's day and wouldn't. "She had the license plate numbers of all four vehicles?"

"Yep. Memorized them. Said she didn't write them down because she thought she was just being paranoid." Hank's mouth twitched. "Must be a hobby of hers, memorizing license plate numbers of suspicious characters like you."

"Hell, she just made up those numbers. You know damned well she—"

Hank withdrew another of his infamous crumpled scraps of paper from a pocket and laid it on the bar. Joe took a bite of his sandwich and had a look. One, two, three, four sets of numbers.

"Are they correct?" Hank asked.

"How would I know? You don't think *I* have nothing better to do than memorize license plate numbers?"

"She got the one on your truck right. I checked with motor vehicles."

The one on his brother's Porsche, too, Joe thought, and probably the other two—Mario's wife's minivan and another friend's econo-box.

"Do you realize," he said to his fellow cop, "how incredibly dull her life must be if she takes the time to memorize license plate numbers? She must think staring at parked cars is high entertainment." He swallowed a mouthful of beer. "What a weirdo."

"You're just ticked because she made you."

"I'm not."

"Your pride is wounded."

"Hank, my pride is not wounded. Name me one cop a woman like that wouldn't have made."

Hank was damned close to grinning. "Admit it, Scarlatti, you underestimated her."

"Okay. I'll admit I underestimated the sick life she leads."

"Beware of stereotyping, my friend. Any sign of Tyhurst yet?"

Joe sighed. "Not a peep."

"He'll show, Joe. My gut says so. I've got reports he's in San Francisco."

"Where's he staying?"

"Don't know—I'm trying to find out. Like I say, he's a free man. He's served his time, says he's reformed."

"Maybe he has."

Hank didn't comment. He didn't need to. He would know Joe didn't believe his own words. Eliot Tyhurst had been born an arrogant, slippery con man and would die an arrogant, slippery con man.

"Rowena Willow put him away for a while," Hank reminded him. "Think about that before you leave her to the bastard. Tyhurst has had three years and then some to figure out a way to pay her back."

Joe slid off the bar stool and started out, but doublebacked for his sandwich. He muttered a goodbye to Hank.

"Joe, where are you going?"

"Obviously," he ground out, "the indirect approach isn't going to work with Ms. Weirdo Willow."

Hank looked worried. "What are you going to do?"

"Try the direct approach."

2

THE NEXT MORNING Rowena remembered to check her street for the undercover cop. She took her tea and the three daily newspapers she received into her third-floor sunroom and arranged a bunch of pillows close to a tall window. Her hair was pinned up, but she was still in her silk bathrobe and had yet to shower and dress.

She scanned the street even before checking the newspaper headlines.

Nothing unusual caught her eye. There was no unidentified vehicle. No glimpse of a dark, solid male figure. Just empty, ordinary parked cars.

Rowena acknowledged a sense of disappointment and wondered at it. What was wrong with her? She wasn't looking for any excitement! Certainly none involving undercover policemen and criminals. She had had enough of that sort of thing three years ago with Eliot Tyhurst.

"I wonder what kind of criminals the police are after up here," she mused aloud to no one. Even Mega and Byte weren't present. Her short-haired tabbies seldom ventured all the way up to the sunroom.

What if her telephone call yesterday had prompted the police to assign someone else to the case? Someone more competent, who wouldn't be so easily spotted by a resident?

Someone, Rowena thought uncomfortably, who wouldn't intrigue her as much.

Dissatisfied with her train of thought, she jumped up and went back downstairs to her kitchen. She popped a fresh peach whole wheat scone into the microwave, her one addition since Aunt Adelaide's day; she'd ordered it from a catalog. She put the scone on a small plate, added a small pat of butter and headed back up to the sunroom, feeling calmer.

Down on the street, a neighbor was buckling her toddler into a car seat. A car was waiting to take her spot. The driver was an elderly man.

Rowena situated herself among her pillows, making herself comfortable, and while the butter melted on her scone, she opened her first newspaper of the morning, the *San Francisco Chronicle*. Her heart stopped. Every muscle in her body tensed. She didn't move. She had no idea how long she stared at the headline.

Tyhurst Returns to San Francisco. In smaller headline print: *Out of prison, mastermind of multimillion-dollar bank fraud say he's reformed*. She couldn't read the article, not until her eyes could focus and her heart had resumed its normal beat. Eliot Tyhurst was out of prison. She hadn't kept track, hadn't known. Hadn't *wanted* to know. After three years, she had finally come to the point where she didn't think about the brilliant, handsome, scheming financial operator she had put in prison. Now he was back.

But Eliot Tyhurst had put *himself* in prison. He was responsible for his actions, not she. She had only unraveled his tangled, corrupt financial system and reported her extraordinary findings to the authorities.

Her mind flashed back to the image of the crowded courtroom when the jury had brought in the guilty verdict. The defendant, formerly one of San Francisco's most prominent and trusted savings and loan owners, had looked at only one person: Rowena Willow. She would never forget how his blue eyes had bored through her. He hadn't said a word. But she knew. He would never forget who had ruined his life.

Now he was a free man.

Reformed, he said. *Rowena Willow, the brilliant financial analyst who brought Tyhurst down,* the newspaper account continued, *couldn't be reached for comment about his release.*

Of course not. Her number was unlisted and if someone rang her doorbell during the day, it was unlikely that she would even hear it. Her concentration was that intense while working. A reporter would have to be intrepid to reach her, and reaching her, it seemed, hadn't been that important. Eliot Tyhurst, she realized, was old news. His return to San Francisco merited a front-page mention only because it was a slow day.

Well, he was bound to be released sometime, she reasoned. And San Francisco was his home. It was logical that he would return to the city. If he had indeed reformed, he had a right to return, start over, mend fences . . . *but I don't want anything to do with him.*

She ate her scone and finished her tea, then had another look out at her street.

Nothing.

Was it possible Hank Ryan had ordered her house watched in the aftermath of Tyhurst's release from prison?

It was. The police had put her through to Ryan when she had called in her warning about the undercover policeman on her street.

Was he worried about her? About any intentions Tyhurst might have toward her?

"No," she said aloud, firmly, reining in her increasingly wild thoughts. "He would have had to tell me."

Surely that was true. She reminded herself that her undercover cop was nowhere to be seen this morning.

She calmed down. Eliot Tyhurst was a footnote in America's financial history; he had served his prison sentence. The police wouldn't—couldn't—spend the time and money worrying about him, about whether he would come after the woman who had put him in jail and cost him millions. They were yesterday's news.

Well, she thought, that would teach her to jump to conclusions based on nothing more than "gut feeling." She had learned the hard way to rely on logic, experience, facts—to always remain in control of her feelings.

Even feelings that insisted against all logic and fact—as hers did now, again—that she had not seen the last of her undercover cop.

JOE COULD HEAR the doorbell to Rowena Willow's mausoleum of a house groan and echo, probably reaching every corner of the bizarre stone building. Hank was right, it looked like a minicastle. The facade was stone, the windows heavily paned and leaded and draped, the door something for a bunch of knights with a battering ram. Weird stuff. He half expected Lurch to open up.

But no one did.

He rang twice more. Rowena Willow, the recluse, had to be home. Where the hell else would she be?

When there was still no response, he pounded on the solid door with his fist in case she just couldn't hear her booming doorbell. At least she would know he meant business.

Not that he gave a damn about Rowena Willow or even, really, this damned job Hank had put him on. It just bugged him that a dingbat like her had spotted him. As Hank had guessed, his pride was wounded. But if his old cop-friend thought that meant Joe was back in the game, he was wrong.

Not a sound came from the castle.

"Hell," Joe muttered through gritted teeth, wondering why he was even bothering. Why not just go on back to Mario's for a beer and burritos?

He went out to the wide sidewalk and glared up at the three-story building, looking for a cracked window, a moving shadow, anything that hinted where she might be. Then he could throw a rock or something and get her attention.

"Hey," he yelled, "anybody home?"

As if Rowena Willow would be anywhere else.

Still nothing.

Joe exhaled in disgust and went back to the massive front door and rang the bell three times in succession, not waiting between rings. He was considering tear gas through a second-floor window when he heard what sounded like someone pounding down a flight of stairs.

He peeked into a narrow side window.

There was a whirling flash of blue, the clicking of locks being thrown free, then the creak of the door as it was drawn open.

Rowena Willow—he assumed it was her—stood before him, breathing hard. She was a hundred times prettier and a thousand times sexier than Joe in four days' watching her had expected.

He was stunned.

He didn't like being stunned. It reduced his sense of control over himself. Even as Rowena Willow's gorgeous, wild, smart blue eyes narrowed on him, he could feel himself putting up mental barriers around himself.

"Don't you answer your door?" he asked.

She looked annoyed. "I just did."

"It took six rings."

"No, only three. I counted."

Her and numbers. "Nope. Six. *I* did the ringing."

She frowned. "I must not have heard . . ." She trailed off, pursing her lips, apparently deciding what she had heard and hadn't heard was none of his business. "What do you want?"

Joe hooked a thumb on a belt loop of his jeans and tried to look as if he dealt with eccentric geniuses every day. *Beautiful* eccentric geniuses. Funny how Hank had neglected to mention Rowena Willow's looks in his briefing.

"Is this how you always treat visitors?" he asked.

"Yes."

Ask a question, he thought, get an answer. "I'm—"

"You're the police officer who has been on a stakeout on my street for the past four days. I spoke to your boss yesterday."

"Hank's not my boss," Joe said, maintaining his good humor despite how much it rankled him that she'd spotted him. He had underestimated Rowena Willow. "And I wasn't on a 'stakeout.' Mind if I come in a minute?"

She sighed, not pleased. "Since you've already blown my concentration—it'll take me hours to get back to where I was—" She stopped herself again, and breathed, "I still need to see some identification."

"Some I.D.," he repeated. "What, when you're not in front of a computer, are you in front of a TV?"

Her lips pursed, and she didn't answer. Her hair, a rich, deep, unusual gold color, was piled up on her head; Joe counted three cloisonné combs and a half-dozen bobby pins at least. Her skin was smooth, flawless, pale. He wondered if it had ever been exposed to the sun. She had a straight nose and those incredible eyes, and a chin that maybe was too strong to put her on a magazine cover. Otherwise she was a classic beauty, tall—almost as tall as he was—and slender. She had on a flowing, azure caftan over cropped black leggings and little tapestry flats.

Joe produced his badge and said, "Name's Scarlatti. Sergeant Joe Scarlatti."

"You're a sergeant?" She sounded dubious. "I would have thought a sergeant would have been more circumspect."

Rub it in, toots, Joe thought. *Go right ahead.* He was a pro. He could take her contempt. What did he care if

Rowena Willow figured she was smarter than he was? Hell, it might be something he could use later on.

She gestured for him to go in ahead of her, which he did. The temperature dropped and the light dimmed; the enormous entry was downright medieval. An open staircase of some dark wood zigzagged up all three floors; a person could fall a long way. The walls were done in some kind of straw matting, and the floor was a dark hardwood with a patterned deep red Persian runner that was so long it would run right out of Joe's place above Mario's Bar & Grill.

A nasty-looking suit of medieval armor complete with spear stood in one corner and an armless statue of some poor bastard stood in another.

"A regular house of horrors," Joe muttered. He should bring Hank for a look-see; maybe he'd quit worrying about what Eliot Tyhurst would do to help-less Rowena Willow.

"We'll talk in the drawing room," she said, opening a set of double doors across the entry from the stairs. "I would offer you something to drink, but five min-utes doesn't give us enough time."

Joe started through the door. "What do you have in here," he said, "poison darts and a couple of mum-mies?"

"I beg your pardon?"

"Never mind."

There was no point, he realized as he crossed the threshold. She wouldn't get his sardonic humor. She'd just take his question seriously, tell him the poison darts and mummies were in another room. *This* room was reserved for stuffed animals. Not the cute, cuddly kind grandmas and grandpas bought for their little grand-kids, either. Rowena Willow's stuffed animals—there were dozens of them—had been alive at one time.

"Quaint," Joe said. He walked over to a curio cabinet of stuffed birds, some ordinary, some rare. There were other cabinets and stands and shelves of larger animals—a raccoon, weasel, gopher, red fox. A few heads—deer, antelope, buffalo—adorned the walls. "Is this what you do with your old boyfriends?"

Rowena Willow eyed him from the middle of the room. "Sergeant, I fail to see your humor."

"Now why doesn't that surprise me?"

"My great-grandfather was a noted taxidermist."

And you, Joe thought, *deliberately use this room to scare off unwanted company.*

"You're wasting your five minutes on trivialities," she pointed out coolly.

He wondered how long her hair was. Midback at least. Did she ever get the urge to pull out all the pins and combs and shake it loose?

"Sergeant," she prompted.

Probably not.

"Just Joe is fine. I'm not here on official business."

That got her interest. She stood next to a small table displaying a single, brightly plumed dead bird. "You're not?"

"Nope. A friend asked me to keep an eye on you in case Eliot Tyhurst decides to exact a little revenge."

It only took a few seconds for his words to sink in. "This friend—you mean Sergeant Ryan?"

Joe shrugged, letting her come to her own conclusions. He didn't want to lie, but he didn't want to rat out Hank, not that his friend didn't deserve it.

"Why would anyone care?" She paused and twisted her fingers together—a gesture of frustration, Joe suspected. He noted the fat sapphire ring on her right hand. There was no engagement ring, no wedding band. "Eliot Tyhurst has made no threats against me. He's served his prison sentence. I don't qualify for police protection."

"Hence, yours truly. I'm on leave from the department—"

"Why?"

A direct woman, but Joe didn't squirm. He pushed back the creeping self-hatred, the memories he had been fighting for too many long months. "Personal reasons."

He waited a moment, giving her a chance to challenge him, press for a better answer, but she didn't, just twisted those fingers together. He had no idea if she understood that he'd said all he planned to say on the subject or if that straight-A mind of hers had figured out that his leave of absence had nothing to do with her case.

"My friend's a good cop," he went on. "He operates a lot on instinct, and his instinct says there could be trouble between you and Tyhurst. He asked me to keep watch, just in case. I've been out here every day for the past four days. I'm not on a twenty-four-hour watch at this point, but I'd guess nothing's happened. Am I right? Tyhurst hasn't been in touch?"

She nodded tightly, then inhaled, tossing her head back, fastening those gorgeous blue eyes on him. Joe let himself notice the soft swell of her breasts under the satiny fabric of her caftan, the pulse beating in her pale throat. Her sensuality was unexpected, overpowering. So was his reaction to it. He had to turn his head, focus on the snarl of the stuffed red fox on a stand beside him. There wasn't a sound in the room. They might have been on the moon, not in the heart of a busy city, atop Telegraph Hill, one of San Francisco's most prestigious and picturesque neighborhoods.

"I gather," Rowena Willow said in a steady voice, "no one thought to ask me what *I* wanted."

"Like I said, it was all very unofficial."

Acknowledging his words with a curt nod, she folded her arms under her breasts and walked slowly over to an enormous window, hung with dark, heavy drapes right out of a Vincent Price movie. With her back to him, she drew the drapes aside and looked out at the street. "You're parked in front of a fire hydrant."

"The privileges of the badge. I'll move if there's a fire, trust me."

"It's your truck—you own it. The other vehicles were borrowed."

"Yep. Hank said you memorized the license plate numbers."

"I wouldn't say I deliberately memorized them. I just made a point of remembering them."

Horsefeathers. She was just trying to intimidate him. "Go ahead," Joe said, "impress me."

She looked around at him, frowning, not one hair out of place.

His attention to every physical detail about her bothered and surprised him. It wasn't professional. It wasn't objective. It wasn't clinical. He didn't do this sort of thing with every woman he met.

"I will do no such thing," she replied stonily.

"Can't remember 'em, huh?" He was being obnoxious and he knew it—but, he told himself, the cop that was still rooted somewhere deep inside him needed to see how Rowena Willow would react.

Not very well. She said calmly, "Your five minutes are up, Sergeant Scarlatti. Have a good morning."

"We didn't finish."

"But we did."

"I haven't gotten to the part about my moving into your little house of horrors here and keeping an eye out on your behalf. It'd be a hell of a lot easier on both of us. I'd have a comfortable place to sit, a kitchen and a bathroom handy. You wouldn't have to stare at parked cars and try to figure out which one's mine."

Color flashed in her milky cheeks. So, he thought, Ms. Weirdo Willow's veins ran with real blood, not ice water. "We don't need to get to that part, Sergeant."

"Are you rejecting my services, ma'am?"

If his sarcasm registered, he couldn't see it. She said, "I don't ever want to see you on this street again unless I call 911 and you're required to come."

"What'll you do if I ignore your wishes?"

"I'll—" She pursed her lips, apparently a habit with her. He wondered if she realized that it made him think about kissing her. Probably not. Not that he *would* kiss her or even wanted to be thinking about doing such a thing, but there it was.

She recovered and went on, "I'll report you to your superiors."

"That'll be fun. You know what they'll tell you?"

"Sergeant—"

"They'll tell you I've got an authority problem. Besides, I don't think I have any superiors. I don't listen to anyone. And like I said, I'm not on active duty." He headed toward the double doors. "You decide you need me, give me a buzz at Mario's Bar & Grill on the waterfront."

"I *won't* need you."

She said it through clenched teeth. Joe grinned. He *had* gotten to her.

"I'll let myself out." He glanced back at her, standing rigid and deliciously beautiful, and nodded to the taxidermy display. "Bet you're wishing these critters could bite. Nice meeting you, Ms. Willow. Mario's Bar & Grill. Got it? Or don't you ever need anything repeated?"

She refused to answer.

Stubborn. But stubbornness—and a distaste for authority—could sometimes get in the way of good judgment. It could even get a person killed, Joe thought. And not always just yourself. He pushed the thought aside as the heavy door thudded behind him. Now wasn't the time for dwelling on past mistakes but considering how the hell not to make new ones.

He was afraid he already had.

ONLY ONCE BEFORE had Rowena been too distracted to work. It was the day Eliot Tyhurst's case had gone to the jury for a verdict. She had wandered and paced in her house until she could stand the tension no longer and had gone down to the courthouse.

Now it was the thought—just the very notion—that *she* had been the target of Sergeant Scarlatti's stakeout that had her too rattled to work. He had been watching her. Protecting her. For four days. Such a prospect had never even occurred to her, even after she had learned Eliot Tyhurst was back in San Francisco.

She felt as if Joe Scarlatti had outwitted her just by knowing something she didn't know. It was, she thought, how *he* would think.

How much did he know about her life?

About her?

She felt the rushing heat of embarrassment—and pure, unadulterated, unwelcome sexual awareness. It was elemental, primitive, surprising, a challenge to her self-control as well as her concentration. And it was unavoidable. Joe Scarlatti was a thickset, compact, physical man who radiated sexuality. Wouldn't any reasonable woman be attracted to him? She knew he'd been attracted to her, if only fleetingly. His appraisal of her had not been from the point of view of a professional, but from that of a man. Had he wondered what she was like in bed? Speculated on her love life?

Her office long abandoned, she heated a bowl of canned vegetable soup—she rarely bothered with lunch—and ate it standing up in the kitchen, trying to regroup.

Would Joe Scarlatti take no for an answer?

No, he wouldn't. He was someone who couldn't resist defying the odds. It was entirely possible she had only succeeded in ensuring he would stay on her case, watching her, *waiting* for something to happen.

But nothing would, she told herself.

Who, she wondered, was she trying to convince?

Her telephone rang, startling her so severely she jumped, spilling a few drops of hot soup onto her hand. She set the bowl down on the counter, still shaking. It was always like that when she was disturbed while she was concentrating—even if on the wrong things. She would be so damned unaware of what was going on around her.

She almost let her machine take the call, as was her general practice during the day, but at the last possible moment she snatched up the wall phone in the kitchen. "Yes?"

"Rowena Willow," a man's silken voice, oddly familiar, said. "Did I get you up from your infamous computer?"

"Who is this?"

"I'm sorry, I thought you might recognize my voice. It's Eliot, Rowena. Eliot Tyhurst."

She forced an inner calm over herself. She couldn't allow a tremor or tightness in her voice to betray her apprehension. "I read that you were in San Francisco. I wish you well, Mr. Tyhurst. Now if you'll excuse me—"

"I'd like to come by and see you."

"I'm very busy."

"I want to thank you, Rowena. Without you, I wouldn't be the man I am today. I wouldn't have seen I was on the wrong path. I grew and changed because of you. I'm a better person because of your courage."

He sounded so sincere. She remembered how polished and deceptively handsome he'd been. Had prison changed him?

"There's no need to thank me," she said quickly. Her stomach had begun to hurt. "I wish you the best, that's all."

"Let me take you to dinner tonight."

"No, I couldn't—"

"Rowena, I *need* to thank you. I need you to believe me. It's important to my total recuperation, my redemption."

She bit down on her lower lip, feeling her rising tension, knowing he would sense it. "Mr. Tyhurst, please understand how difficult this is for me. I don't want to see you."

"I do understand. That's the whole point. And call me Eliot, please. Rowena, how can I convince you I'm a new man? How can I convince *anyone* if not you?"

Rowena twisted the phone cord, wondering what Joe Scarlatti would have her do if he were here. Turn the phone over to him? Let him handle Eliot Tyhurst?

She handled her own life, her own problems. It had *always* been that way for her.

Her hesitation provided the former banker his opening. "Then you do understand. I'll pick you up at seven." And he added matter-of-factly, "I know where you live."

JOE SCARLATTI MET Hank for a hot dog and soda at a street vendor's in front of Eliot Tyhurst's old savings and loan downtown. It was located in a flashy modern building famous on San Francisco's skyline.

"I want everything we've got on that SOB," Joe said. "Whatever you can get me, I want."

"Will do."

"Unofficially."

"Sure."

"And I'm not saying I'm really on this case."

"There is no case," Hank said.

"Right." Joe squirted mustard over his sauerkraut. "One more thing."

Hank, the turncoat, was grinning, having sucked Joe Scarlatti back into the world he had been trying for six months to leave behind. "What's that, Joe?"

"I'm going to stay on Rowena Willow," he said, "and if she catches me this time, I'll turn in my badge for good and become partners with Mario and serve drinks and greasy sandwiches for the next forty years."

"I won't hold you to that."

"What, you have no faith in me?"

"No, Joe, I've got all the faith in the world in you, but Rowena Willow—she rooted out Tyhurst, didn't she? What makes you think she won't root out a burnt-out cop she's met, decided she doesn't like, doesn't trust and wants out of her life?"

Joe stuffed a few strands of loose sauerkraut back into his hot-dog bun. "You just watch me."

3

TWO HOURS AFTER Eliot Tyhurst had called, Rowena ducked through her back door and courtyard and slipped through a wrought-iron gate to a side alley, her usual shortcut around the block. The scent of roses lingered. Aunt Adelaide had planted scores of them in the little courtyard, and Rowena felt a rush of nostalgia and pain. Her aunt had done her best in difficult circumstances, raising a child long, long after she herself had chosen to have no children. If Rowena's parents had lived...if Aunt Adelaide had been less eccentric, more social, even understood the basic needs of an extraordinarily bright, lonely, grieving little girl...if Rowena had been less inwardly drawn herself...

But that was all in the past. Aunt Adelaide was gone, and her parents were gone. Rowena had forgiven her, and them, and even herself.

Did she now owe Eliot Tyhurst her forgiveness?

Was it hers to offer? He hadn't fleeced her of a single cent, and she believed people deserved a second chance. A judicial system couldn't work properly if society didn't allow ex-convicts an opportunity for a fresh start.

And yet that was so much easier to believe in principle than to act upon in real life.

She walked quickly down Telegraph Hill, toward the water, enjoying the feel of the warm sunshine. It was a clear, glorious October day. She had changed into knee-length walking shorts, a cropped top and walking shoes. Given the sensitivity of her skin to the sun, she'd put on a big floppy hat that hid most of her face. Her jaunts through the city, although relatively infrequent lately given the mountains of projects she'd agreed to undertake, were always welcome. She loved San Francisco's steep hills and stunning architecture, the clanging of its streetcars, the blaring of its foghorns. Everywhere there was another incredible, breathless view of the bay, the ocean, the Golden Gate Bridge.

Enjoying the scenery, however, did nothing to distract Rowena from thinking about Eliot Tyhurst and Sergeants Hank Ryan and Joe Scarlatti. They presented a knotty problem indeed, not the sort she was accustomed to solving. She was comfortable among numbers and complex financial systems, analyzing companies and trends and markets for her business clients. She had never claimed ease among the male of the human species.

She walked and walked, trying to focus on the scenery, trying to tell herself she wasn't headed where she knew full well she was headed. But soon she could feel the dampness of the waterfront in the air, feel the cool breeze off the bay on her face. The wind grew stronger, and she had to hold on to her hat. Automatically, because this was her city and she knew every street and alley of it, and because she had called up the address on her computer, she turned down the street where Mario's Bar & Grill was located.

It was in an older, Victorian-style building with a simple sign giving its name.

Rowena hesitated, wishing she'd opted for an outfit that would give her a more commanding presence. Or hadn't come at all.

But she had come.

She went through the door—oak and frosted glass—and immediately fought a rush of emotion at the smell of popcorn and sourdough bread, at the sound of laughter and soft jazz, of a life she didn't lead. She squared her shoulders and approached the gleaming bar. The place wasn't crowded; it was between lunch and dinner. A plump man in a dark green apron was polishing beer glasses with a clean white cloth.

"Help you?" he asked.

"I'm looking for Joe Scarlatti."

The man set down his cloth and eyed her. "Won't he kick himself for not being around for once. Do I know you?"

"My name's Rowena Willow."

"You're the one put that slime-mold Tyhurst in jail. Yeah, I know you. Joe didn't tell me—"

"Eliot Tyhurst put himself in jail," she corrected.

"Right, right. Mario Scarlatti." He put out a hand, which Rowena shook briefly across the bar. "Joe's cousin. Go out the door and holler for him. He probably followed you down here."

Rowena felt a surge of heat. "But I told him—he's not supposed to follow me."

"Mistake number one. Never tell Joe Scarlatti what to do. His mama gave up when he was two years old."

"It wasn't his choice—"

"All the more reason not to do what you said."

"Did he tell you—are you sure—" She stopped, disgusted with her sputtering, and marched over to the door, kicking it open with one foot.

Joe Scarlatti was tying the laces of his beat-up running shoe on the top step of the landing. He grinned up at her. "Well, well, if it isn't our eccentric genius. Care for an afternoon beer, Ms. Willow?"

"Did you follow me?" she demanded.

"You're the one who knows everything. You tell me."

"You have no right—"

"Mario tell you I followed you? Don't believe everything he says. He's trying to get me into trouble because he's sick of me hanging around." Scarlatti finished tying his shoe and straightened up. "What're you doing, checking up on me?"

"No, I . . ."

"You what?"

She felt ridiculous. And angry. Scarlatti must have followed her. What was more, her reaction to him was just as violently sensual as it had been that morning—as it had been since she'd spotted him five days ago and had only *imagined* him. In person, up close, for real, he was even more overpowering than glimpsed, half-imagined, from her third-floor sunroom.

"I've got to go," she mumbled, starting past him.

He grabbed her upper arm, effectively stopping her in her tracks. His grip was strong, but not harsh. A terrible, wanting ache spread through her at the feel of it. Her mouth went dry. She would never respond this way to Eliot Tyhurst, reformed or not, but it was he, not Sergeant Joe Scarlatti, who had invited her to dinner.

But Joe Scarlatti, she thought, represented a greater threat to her personal security—her sense of control over her life—than Eliot Tyhurst ever could. She knew that now. It was why her attraction bothered her. A man like Scarlatti could make her forget her purpose in life, her responsibilities, the unintended lessons her parents' destructive love for each other had taught her.

"At least have something to drink first," Scarlatti said.

Rowena found herself nodding. Acquiescing. She didn't know why, except that she *was* thirsty, and it was a long way back up to Telegraph Hill—and she somehow felt she should be here. She had learned to trust her intuition. No one, least of all her, could explain the unique blend of intuition, memory and raw intelligence that permitted her to know things the way she did. Even if she didn't yet completely understand why, she'd had to come here.

Mario had a beer waiting on the bar for Scarlatti. Rowena could see the questions in the older man's eyes, but he said nothing to his cousin. She asked for mineral water with a twist of lime.

"Will you take seltzer?" Mario asked. "Same thing, my opinion, just not as fancy a name."

It wasn't the same, but Rowena didn't argue. "That's fine."

The younger, more fit Scarlatti slid onto the bar stool. Rowena noticed that his leg muscles were as thick and solid as she'd imagined yesterday when he'd climbed out of his truck. She didn't sit down. The sergeant frowned at her and told her to sit.

"Thank you, I'll stand."

"If I told you to stand, would you sit?"

"I'm not being obstinate."

"Then you're being self-conscious. Sit down, for Pete's sake. You're making me nervous."

She very much doubted that, but she eased halfway onto the bar stool, somewhere between sitting and standing. Mario brought out her seltzer with lime, and a fake-wood bowl of pretzels and mixed nuts.

"Finished computing for the day?" Joe asked.

"I never really got started. There were too many interruptions."

"What, one little visit from a cop blows your whole day?"

"Coupled with an unsettling phone call, yes."

Scarlatti was silent. His eyes, however, were dark and alert, ready to seize upon anything she dared give away.

"I'm having dinner with Eliot Tyhurst tonight," Rowena said quietly.

"The hell you are."

"It's his way of making peace with what he did. He says he's reformed. He needs to have me accept his new self. I was a party to his downfall. I might not owe him a second chance, but I owe society—"

"What kind of garbage is that? Tyhurst can get his second chance without having dinner with you."

She thrust her jaw out stubbornly. Scarlatti's domineering attitude was just the push she needed to convince herself to go ahead with the dinner. "I can't *not* have dinner with him."

"Yeah, you can." He was not succeeding in dissuading her. He drank some of his beer and told her arrogantly, "You call him up, you tell him you've made other plans and you make sure you're not home tonight in case he doesn't listen." Scarlatti set his beer firmly on the worn, smooth bar. "Better yet, *I'll* call him."

She sipped her seltzer, which was refreshing if not good. It gave her something to do besides stare at this intriguing, infuriating man and acknowledge how easily he could get to her. "I don't have his number."

"You found millions of dollars he'd stashed away. You can find his number."

Rowena stiffened. "You're not my keeper, Sergeant Scarlatti."

"And you're a romantic, Rowena Willow, if you believe Eliot Tyhurst has changed. You live up in your castle tower and don't know squat about the real world."

"I'd rather be a bit of a romantic than a cynic. Someone who has paid his debt to society deserves a chance to prove he's rehabilitated. Society cannot function if that person isn't given that chance."

Scarlatti didn't even look at her. "You breathe real air up in that ivory tower of yours?"

Rowena was insulted. She refused to say a word until he looked at her. When he did, she almost wanted to look away, so powerful was his pull on her. But she forced herself to fasten her gaze on him. She set her jaw.

He didn't flinch.

"I will make my own decisions," she told him.

As she started up, she placed her hand lightly on the lip of the bar for support. Scarlatti covered it with his, holding her steady. "Why tell me about Tyhurst if you're not going to listen to my advice?"

"Was that advice? It sounded more like an order to me. I came, Sergeant," she said icily, "as a simple courtesy to you and Sergeant Ryan. You anticipated Eliot Tyhurst would contact me, and he has. I believed it my duty to inform you, just as I believe it my duty to have dinner with Mr. Tyhurst this evening."

Scarlatti still hadn't released her. His hand was warm and strong, and she could feel the calluses. In a sudden, totally out-of-place thought, she wondered what his hands would feel like on her breasts, the curve of her hip.

She *must* be going out of her mind. Perhaps she needed a vacation. Or more work. Lots more work, to keep her mind productively occupied.

"You could have called the department and left a message for me," he said, watching her closely. His eyes narrowed. "Something wrong?"

"No!"

She dismissed the vivid, paralyzing thought of him making love to her. She was in shock. How could her mind be so treacherous? It wasn't that she was sexually repressed or considered attraction to a man unhealthy, just that she considered her attraction to *this* man out of proportion and potentially dangerous. He was a detective on leave from the San Francisco police department. She was a financial whiz. They had nothing in common. It wasn't sensible to respond so heatedly to a man so clearly not right for her, and she had vowed to herself that she would be sensible not only in matters of finance, but of the heart.

With tremendous self-discipline—which she hoped he couldn't detect—she tossed her head back haughtily. "Why should I waste the police's time with something unofficial—" she eyed him significantly "—and so *trivial?*"

"Cute, Ms. Willow." He let her go, and she could breathe again. "Real cute."

This time when she left, he didn't stop her.

Until she reached the door.

"What time is Tyhurst picking you up?"

"Seven. Do *not* interfere, Sergeant."

His grin was intentionally sexy, challenging. "Sweetheart, you won't even know I'm there."

ROWENA SENSED Joe Scarlatti's presence the rest of the afternoon and into the evening.

She sensed it when she was putting on a slim chocolate brown skirt and cream-colored silk blouse. She sensed it when she slipped on her stockings and combed her hair and repinned it and clipped on sapphire earrings. She sensed it when she paced in the entry before seven o'clock, hearing only the sounds of her footsteps echoing in the cavernous house.

She'd checked the street periodically, but there was no sign of Scarlatti.

Yet he was out there, somewhere. She knew it.

Could *feel* it.

Aunt Adelaide's suit of armor stood silent, almost like an old friend. Rowena hadn't yet bothered redecorating the first two floors of the house since her aunt's death. She wasn't sure why: she could certainly afford it. She loathed the taxidermy room. She planned eventually to donate its displays to a museum, although the room came in handy to discourage certain kinds of visitors. After all, she could have taken Joe Scarlatti out to the courtyard to talk.

The doorbell rang. She answered it at once.

Scarlatti strode into the entry. He had on a black pullover and black canvas pants, worn and loose. Burnt-out or not, he looked very tough and competent. And annoyed. "How come you answer on the first ring when you think it's Eliot Tyhurst and it took me six rings to rouse you this morning?"

"I was working and you were uninvited," Rowena replied coolly, "just as you are now. What are you doing here?"

"Just seeing if you were going through with dinner with this ex-con who bilked the American people out of millions."

"He served his time."

"He'd have gotten more time if he'd held up a gas station."

"I have no control over the criminal justice system."

"Yeah, well." He left it at that and gave her a long, deliberately obvious head-to-toe once-over that finished at her face. "My, my. Makeup, even. Eliot Tyhurst gets the full treatment and I get sensible shoes and a floppy hat."

"It's after dark now, and I burn easily, and we won't be walking. Not that I have to justify myself to you."

"How old are you?"

His non sequitur caught her off guard. "What does that have to do with anything?"

"You're young for an eccentric genius, aren't you?"

"Eliot Tyhurst will be arriving any minute. I would prefer not to have to introduce you as my bodyguard."

"I'm not a bodyguard, sweetheart." He moved toward her, across the invisible line that marked the boundary to her space, invading it with his primitive heat. "You couldn't afford to pay me what I'd charge to protect you, even if you sold off every stuffed bird and horror-house trinket in this place and raided every mutual fund you own. I'm a cop. I'm not in this for you."

She believed him. Joe Scarlatti, she thought, was a hard and complex man, and she dared not underestimate him. The only way to deal with him was on a basic, elemental level.

She raised her chin slightly and peered into his eyes, which were hot and dark and challenging. She kept hers cool and objective. "I stand corrected. Nevertheless, you're not here in an official capacity and I have a right to ask you to leave. Please do so."

He didn't back off a millimeter. "Call off your dinner, Rowena."

"Is that an order?"

"A suggestion."

"Are you going to follow me?"

He shook his head. "Can't risk it. You're on your own tonight."

"Fine."

"Dammit—"

"I'm choosing the restaurant. He doesn't know that yet, but I am. We'll be at the Meridien. I didn't want anything too small and intimate."

"More chance someone will recognize him."

"Precisely why I chose such a public spot. If his motives are suspect, he'll have a hard time acting on them with witnesses who not only can provide a description of him, but his name, too."

"What about transportation?"

"I'm driving."

Scarlatti couldn't hide his surprise. "You have a car?"

"I intend to drive his," she said. "Look, he's going to be here. Duck into the drawing room until I'm gone, then let yourself out."

He gave her a nasty, sexy smile. "Is that an order?"

She smiled back, just as nastily, maybe not so sexily, and refused to act on the urge to step away from him. "Give it up, Sergeant. You care about Tyhurst seeing you more than I do. You know why? You're not interested in protecting me from him. Neither is Sergeant Ryan. You're after Tyhurst for reasons that have nothing to do with me personally."

Something—she didn't know what—made his eyes flash. "Tell me, do you ever doubt one of your own opinions or are you always so obnoxiously sure of yourself?"

"My only question," she continued, as if he hadn't spoken, "is *why* an ordinary cop like you would want Tyhurst so much."

"Lady, I'm a lot of things, but ordinary isn't one of them."

She ignored the implication of his words. Or pretended to. She was intensely aware of every millimeter of him. "I'll find out," she promised.

The doorbell rang, and Scarlatti quietly—if not obediently—slipped into the drawing room.

JOE FELT hundreds of beady glass eyes on him in the dark, overly populated drawing room. Rowena Willow was much more of a handful than he had anticipated. He had almost lost her this afternoon when she took off to Mario's. He should have checked right in the beginning for a back exit from her mausoleum. And he should have guessed someone so independent, so damned alone, would jump all over a dinner invitation from an ex-con she'd helped nail. She was giving him a second chance. She owed society. Hell. The lady was bored out of her mind.

And out to show him.

That had been a mistake, he thought. He shouldn't have got her goat the way he had. She certainly wasn't acquiescent.

And she suspected his motives for watching her weren't entirely unselfish.

Joe *had* taken the case because of Tyhurst and not because of any real concern for Rowena Willow. But Rowena didn't have to know that. It was none of her business that his grandparents weren't financial geniuses, that Tyhurst had been able to rob them blind.

For a reclusive workaholic, she had a way of stirring things up.

Admit it, Scarlatti. You haven't felt this alive in months.

He wasn't admitting anything.

He pressed his ear to the thick double doors and listened.

"Rowena—my heavens, you look lovely."

Joe felt bile rise in his throat at the sound of the bastard's smooth voice. But he had to agree with Tyhurst on that one point—Rowena did look damned attractive. He hoped, however, the crooked banker was responding to her in a more objective, clinical, calculated manner than Joe himself did. Rowena Willow made him think about sex. It was that damned simple and probably would surprise the hell out of her if she knew. And maybe scare her into being less confrontational. Maybe if he *were* on official business his professionalism would have kicked into gear.

He silently cursed Hank Ryan for getting him into this mess, although he knew if he hadn't been on leave, he wouldn't have been free to take the crazy case of Rowena Willow and the banker. His leave of absence was his own choice. What else could a man do who blamed himself for his partner and best friend's death? After almost a year, it still ate at him, day and night. He would never forgive himself, never be the man he was before Matt's death.

He couldn't let anyone else trust him the way Matt Lee had come to trust him. Matt had trusted him with his life, and Joe had failed him. There were no two ways about it. That was the plain, raw truth.

Joe heard Rowena awkwardly thank Tyhurst, obviously unaccustomed to getting compliments on her appearance. She needed to get out more, he thought. She'd get used to it fast if she did. "I thought the Meridien would be nice tonight," she said.

Tyhurst laughed softly. "No, no, I have a special place all picked out."

Joe stiffened, placed a hand on the door latch. He shoved thoughts of Matt and the past deep to the back of his mind. He was ready to act.

"Where?" Rowena asked.

Good, Joe thought, but he didn't for a minute think she'd asked on his account, so he would be able to follow. She was asking because she wanted to know.

But Eliot Tyhurst said, "On the water—you'll love it."

Argue with him, Joe urged silently. *Argue with him the way you do with me.* She didn't say a word, and the front door creaked.

Joe raced across the dark drawing room to the windows. Standing to one side, he carefully pulled back the drapes and peered out at the quiet, pretty street.

Eliot Tyhurst had one hand on Rowena's elbow. She shook loose, subtly. He was a tall, lean, handsome bastard. His suit alone would set Joe back a month's rent with Mario. Tyhurst was educated and sophisticated, just the kind of man for Rowena Willow, if he weren't also a crook.

Joe saw her glance back toward the drawing room window. Her smile was forced, her face pale and tight in the harsh streetlight. Joe reminded himself that Tyhurst was a white-collar criminal, not the armed-and-dangerous variety Joe dealt with on the streets. It was unlikely Rowena was in any physical danger.

Then Tyhurst opened the passenger door, and she got in.

They weren't going to the Meridien. She wasn't driving.

Joe got out the keys to his truck.

The hell she was on her own.

4

Rowena sat stiffly beside Eliot Tyhurst. He seemed unchanged, at least outwardly, by his prison experience, but she reminded herself he was a newly released convict. She shouldn't be fooled by the scent of his expensive cologne, by the sleek cut of his suit, by the neatness of his tawny-colored hair. He seemed as pulled together and sophisticated as he had at his trial, before conviction and prison. Rowena was uncertain why she'd climbed into his car, why she'd let him take control of their destination. Impulse? Curiosity? A way of getting back at Joe Scarlatti for doubting her ability to handle herself? She just didn't know.

She hardly spoke until they were on the Golden Gate Bridge. "We're going to Marin?" she asked.

"Yes, is that all right? I thought it would be quieter, less chance for either of us to be recognized."

"It's fine. I haven't been out this way in a long time."

Tyhurst nodded as if he understood. Other than completely ignoring her wishes for the evening, whether or not he had done so deliberately, he was behaving like a perfect gentleman. Of course, his smooth manner had contributed to his ability to bilk hundreds of people out of their life savings. They had entrusted their money to him with the same blind faith that had led Rowena into his car. Nothing would happen to her, she told herself. She wasn't afraid of Eliot Tyhurst. At worst he was a con man. A computer criminal. A slick white-collar operator. It wasn't as if she were trapped in a car with a sociopathic killer.

And at the time, she had to admit, climbing into his car with him had seemed preferable to crying out to Joe Scarlatti for help. Already she regretted her plaintive look back toward the house. How had he interpreted it? *Surely* he had been watching from the drawing room window.

Well, she thought, *now you're on your own*.

Wasn't that what she wanted? It certainly was what she was accustomed to. What she'd worked for, struggled for. She had learned at a young age to rely on her own wits and abilities.

Tyhurst wound the small, comfortable car—nothing as ostentatious as what he probably used to drive—into the picturesque village of Sausalito and parked at a restaurant that offered a spectacular view of San Francisco across the bay. Rowena forgot her uneasiness as she got out of the car. She absorbed the beauty of the skyline glittering in the distance, the freshness of the wind in her face, the freedom of being away from her house and computer.

Eliot Tyhurst materialized beside her. "Stunning, isn't it?"

He was, indeed, a handsome man, she thought. Refined, polished. And there was a sadness in his eyes that intrigued her. Yet she felt no rush of sensual heat the way she did with the police sergeant.

She smiled. "Yes, it is."

"I requested a table by the window. Shall we?"

He put out his arm, and short of being rude, Rowena had little choice but to take it. She was mildly surprised by his obvious strength. Had he taken up pumping iron in prison? She felt self-conscious. All she needed now was an astute news photographer to jump out of the shrubs and snap their picture.

The restaurant was intimate and elegant, with a small bar and no more than a dozen tables arranged in front of huge floor-to-ceiling windows overlooking the bay. Rowena stood back while Tyhurst took over, suave and at ease with himself and his surroundings. He chatted with the maître d' without any of the awkwardness she might have expected from a man fresh out of prison.

He pulled out Rowena's chair for her at their candlelit table. "Thank you for being here," he whispered in her ear. "Not everyone would have trusted me."

Rowena licked her lips as he sat across from her. "I did encounter opposition from one friend who—who suggested you could be out for revenge." She'd managed not to trip over her description of Joe Scarlatti as a friend.

Tyhurst nodded grimly, the sadness drifting from his eyes to his mouth. In the soft light of the restaurant she saw now that lines had formed at the corners of his eyes and etched into his forehead. The cockiness he'd displayed during his trial was gone. Maybe he had changed. "That friend doesn't understand what you did for me. I'm not a bad person, Rowena. I admit I resented you for a long time. I wanted desperately to believe you and you alone were responsible for my downfall. I kept telling myself that if you hadn't interfered, nothing would have happened. If you'd just left me alone, I believed I would have been able to keep my clients' money safe—that in the end everything would have worked out."

"Is that what you still believe?"

"No!" His eyes widened, appalled. "Oh, no. I finally came to understand that I and I alone was responsible for my own downfall. If I'd been left alone, I only would have destroyed more people. I had an inflated view of my ability to make things work out. I refused for a long time to see the true nature of my activities. Arrogance and overconfidence led me to use my clients' money for my own gain. It was wrong of me not to fully inform them, even if I never really intended them to suffer."

"You broke the law," Rowena reminded him.

"That, too."

"What do you want now?"

He looked at her. He seemed weary, filled with regrets. His shoulders sagged. "A fresh start."

She opened her mouth to answer but a movement near the bar drew her eye.

Joe Scarlatti had climbed onto a bar stool. The bartender was sliding him a tall glass of what looked like beer. Rowena felt her heart thump wildly in her chest.

"Is something wrong?" Tyhurst asked, concerned.

"What? Oh—oh, I'm sorry. No, nothing's wrong. I'm just not used to being out in the evening. It's nothing you said."

But she watched as Scarlatti turned in his seat, his back to the black-wood bar. His eyes sought out hers. Deliberately. Overpoweringly. She had to fight to pull her gaze away.

Why had he followed her?

How?

That look she'd given him. He had interpreted it as helpless and frightened. In need of him.

Eliot Tyhurst was frowning. "Rowena?"

She made herself smile. He didn't know about her unofficial protector. She had nothing to worry about.

Except for Joe Scarlatti himself. She had no idea what he would do. None. His actions were completely unpredictable. She didn't like things—including people—she couldn't predict.

Mercifully their waiter intervened, and she ordered a glass of champagne. "To celebrate," she said, almost as smoothly as Tyhurst himself. And she smiled at him. "To celebrate new beginnings."

Relief and pleasure washed over his face, and instead of opting for a second glass, he asked the waiter to bring a bottle of champagne. Their discussion of what vintages were available gave Rowena the opportunity to pull herself together. Scarlatti was going to make an evening of it. He'd sit there all through dinner, an immense distraction.

Suddenly she wished she had stayed home and played solitaire on her computer.

She noticed Eliot's eyes on her and quickly opened her menu. "Have you been here before?" she asked.

"No, but I understand the menu's limited but very good—everything's fresh."

And probably will taste terrific after months of prison food. What did she think she was doing out with an ex-con?

From the look of him, Scarlatti was wondering the same thing. As if she couldn't be trusted to be out on her own. She knew he thought she was too reclusive, too naive, too *weird*.

Tyhurst's eyes got a faraway look, and as if he had read her thoughts, he said, "But don't expect me to be a good judge—what I consider acceptable cuisine after my ordeal would surprise you."

If not for his easy manner, his almost self-deprecating tone and his soft, warm eyes, Rowena might have winced. Yet his words seemed without edge or self-pity.

She snuck a peek at Scarlatti. He had turned back to the bar and was engaged in conversation with the bartender. He looked comfortable there. His casual attire didn't even seem out of place, despite the more formal dress of those who had come for dinner.

Did he know more about the Eliot Tyhursts of the world than Rowena did?

He assumed he did. Tyhurst had been to prison. Ergo, Scarlatti knew more about him.

Their champagne came, and they ordered—Tyhurst the grilled salmon, Rowena a pasta dish—and toasted to knew beginnings. Finally he said, "Tell me about yourself, Rowena. I know so very little."

Awkwardness inundated her, and she looked quickly out the window, noting the lights of boats bobbing on the choppy water. She didn't know what to say. Although introspective by nature, she was not self-absorbed. And she didn't know how much she wanted Eliot Tyhurst to know about her. What should she tell him?

"My work is going very well," she said. "I recently received a complicated assignment from a New England company that looks interesting—"

Tyhurst stopped her, shaking his head indulgently. "I want to know about *you*. What makes Rowena Willow tick?"

Nothing came to her. Absolutely nothing. Was it because Sergeant Scarlatti was just yards away? Had his nearness left her tongue-tied? "That's not an easy question to answer."

"You don't trust me."

"It's not that. Mr. Tyhurst—"

"Eliot. Please call me Eliot."

"Eliot—" she tried to smile when she said it "—to be truthful, I don't know whether I should trust you or not. I don't know you well enough. You're making a new beginning for yourself. I wouldn't presume to judge you. It's simply not my place."

The hurt look vanished from his handsome face. "That's a start."

A start toward what?

Toward giving him the second chance he needed, she told herself. Nothing more.

"I'm afraid," she went on, "that if I can't talk about my work, I never know what to say when someone asks about me. My Aunt Adelaide—she raised me—taught me not to talk too much about myself, not just because it's vain but because Willows aren't always understood. I—well, I come from an eccentric family."

"So I've heard," Eliot said gently. "Suppose you just start with the basics and we'll go from there."

She smiled, relaxing. "I have two cats, and I live alone."

"You have an interesting house," he said, almost as if he were coaching her. He sipped his champagne. She did likewise.

"Oh, yes. My great-grandfather, Cedric Willow, built it. Some people say I'm a lot like him and . . ." She couldn't go on, and it had nothing to do with any reluctance to talk about herself. Her stomach was twisted with tension, and it was all because Scarlatti was there at the bar, watching her again, and she couldn't stop thinking about him. "Excuse me a moment, won't you?"

Tyhurst's face clouded again, but he said smoothly, "Of course."

She rushed toward the ladies' room, right past Scarlatti, stifling an impulse to mutter something to him.

The ladies' room was small and scented with potpourri, papered with tiny roses. Rowena patted her face with cold water, careful not to smear her makeup. Her eyes looked huge, her cheeks flushed, her lips full. She was out of her element. Cops and ex-cons—the closest she usually came to them was on a computer game, or reading about them in the papers, or in a book. She didn't have *dinner* with them. She didn't have them *spying* on her.

This wasn't her life. Not tonight.

What she had to do, she decided, was get through dinner with Eliot Tyhurst and thus show Joe Scarlatti her judgment was sound and she didn't need him following her around, and in the morning she'd get her life back.

It was a good, simple, solid plan.

Resolved to follow it, she swept out of the ladies' room.

And almost landed in Joe Scarlatti's arms.

He had the receiver of a wall pay phone in one hand. "You've been talking a blue streak," he said to her, his eyes dark, penetrating, angry. "You telling the guy your life story? Eat up and go home."

"He's trying to get me to talk about myself," she said, "and I am not 'talking a blue streak.'"

"What's he need to know?"

"He says everything. Maybe he's just being courteous."

Scarlatti slammed the phone down and swung back around at her. "And maybe he's a goddamned crook."

She set her jaw. "You can go home now, Sergeant."

"Did I ever say I was working for you?"

"I'll have you arrested for harassment."

He gave a low, arrogant laugh.

"I can take care of myself," she said.

"Yeah," he said, "that's why you drove and that's why you're at the Meridien. Or don't you *know* where the hell you are?"

"If we were anywhere else," she said through clenched teeth, "I would slap you across the face."

He didn't back off. "You'll have your chance."

"Go home."

She started off, but his hand shot out, grabbing her by the wrist, spinning her around to his chest. If Eliot Tyhurst decided to go to the men's room, he would see them, and yet Rowena's head spun with the thrill of the risk she was taking, of the masculine smell of the hard cop whose breath she could feel hot on her face.

"Let me take you out of here," he said in a low, tight voice. "Now."

"I can't—"

His mouth came down on hers with such sudden fierceness Rowena didn't have a chance to let out a cry of surprise, only to open her lips. He took full advantage. His tongue plunged into her mouth, tasting her, warning her. She felt herself sinking against him, responding. An agonizing desire spread through her.

He pulled away as fiercely as he'd come to her. His gaze swept over her. Then he straightened. He seemed at the very edge of his self-control. "You'd better hit the ladies' room again before you head back."

And he stalked down the short hall and around the corner into the restaurant.

This time Rowena did as he advised. Looking at her reflection in the mirror, she knew what he'd meant. Her nipples were visibly hard under her filmy blouse, her eyes dusky with pent-up desire, her lipstick smudged. The taste of him was still on her tongue.

What if she'd asked him to drive her home?

They would never have got that far. They'd have had to stop somewhere and make love.

It was that way between them.

She quickly redid her lipstick and hoped the restaurant's dim light would prevent her dinner date from noticing any other evidence of what she'd been doing on her trip to the ladies' room.

Passing Joe Scarlatti was no mean feat. His smoky gaze settled on her, told her that he wanted her—that he would have her. She felt its searing heat as she wove through the tables, now crowded with diners, back to Eliot Tyhurst.

"Is everything all right?" he asked.

"Yes, fine."

Their dinner arrived, and Rowena, grateful for the distraction, raved perhaps more than was necessary. Tyhurst seemed pleased. But before he could resume asking her about herself, she said, "What do you plan to do now that you've served your sentence?"

He shrugged. "I'm not sure. I'm thinking over my options." He had, she recalled, declared himself bankrupt three years ago. "I'll find something to do. Something positive, I hope."

Rowena wanted to believe him. Part of her *did* believe him. "With your talents," she said, "you have a whole host of positive opportunities to choose from."

"Do I?"

"Of course."

He smiled sadly. "You're so naive, Rowena—or maybe I'm too jaded. I hope..." He paused, looking pained. "I hope I'll find other people as willing to forgive and forget as you are."

"I know you're barred from certain financial activities for life, but I should think if you've served your sentence and take a little time to prove your good intentions, someone will give you a second chance."

"Let's hope so."

There was an edge to his words this time. She wondered if it had more to do with his fear of the future than his regrets about the past. But he launched into a discussion of how San Francisco had changed in the three years he'd been away, and Rowena was grateful he didn't insist on having her talk about herself. Still, she ate her pasta as quickly as she could, telling herself she wasn't taking the sergeant's advice.

He was still at the bar, his back to her. Every time she stole a look at him, she could taste his mouth on hers, feel the hot probing of his tongue. Was his kiss deliberate? Impulsive?

Did she dare trust him any more than Eliot Tyhurst?

It didn't matter. Whatever he was after, *she* wanted a chance to kiss him. To leave him as distracted and taken aback and aching as she was.

After she and Tyhurst had finished their main courses, Rowena agreed to a cup of coffee, but refused dessert. And she insisted on paying for her own dinner. This time she didn't just go along with him as she had with his choice of restaurant and decision to drive. There'd be no more impulsive behavior, no more indulging curiosity or a ridiculous need not to show weakness to a burnt-out San Francisco cop.

When she got up to leave, she saw that Joe Scarlatti had vacated his seat at the bar.

Where was he?

There was no sign of his battered truck out in the parking lot, or of him. Rowena wondered fleetingly if he'd taken her advice and had gone home. *You're on your own again*, she thought, but quickly reminded herself that she'd always been on her own. A few days of Joe Scarlatti in her life hadn't changed a thing.

She spoke little on their way back across the Golden Gate Bridge, into the view that had so transfixed her from the other side of the bay. Glancing at Tyhurst, she tried to imagine what it would be like to pick up the pieces of her life after a prison sentence, however brief. Would she fare any better than Eliot Tyhurst? Could she be as magnanimous to the person who had put her there? *If* that was what he was being.

She couldn't tell. She was no judge of people, and Eliot Tyhurst was particularly hard to read. She watched him as he drove with both hands on the wheel, his eyes narrowed on the road like a teenager just learning to drive. It had been a while, she realized, since he had driven a car. *Thanks to me.* No, thanks to himself.

"Would you like me to walk you to your door?" he asked when he pulled up to her house. It did look like a dreary old castle at night.

"No, thanks. I can manage."

She pushed open the car door and started out.

He leaned toward her, touched her shoulder. "Is there anyone special in your life, Rowena?"

A chill ran up her spine. She turned to look at him. She had one foot out on the pavement. "Lots of people."

"I lost my wife over this ordeal. She was horrified at my—how did she put it? My 'unconscionable behavior.' As if I were a mass murderer." He sighed, letting his hand fall away. "It's not easy being alone."

She climbed out of his car and looked around at him, feeling a small surge of sympathy. "I guess it's not so hard when it's all you've known."

In a few moments, she was on her doorstep and Eliot Tyhurst was gone.

The door echoed in the cavernous entry when she shut it behind her. She peeked outside. There was no sign of Joe Scarlatti or his truck. Was he more competent than she'd given him credit for? Or just less interested, less concerned about her safety?

Mega and Byte floated down the carpeted stairs and rubbed against her leg, welcoming her back.

"Ahh, kitties," she said, "you don't know how good it is to be home."

But she froze, hearing the loud rumble of an old truck engine outside her door. Looking through the window, she saw Joe Scarlatti's battered truck parallel-parking in a space that was clearly insufficient for its bulk. He didn't give up. He just parked it at a sharp angle—a thorough eyesore on her attractive, upmarket street—and climbed out with a big bundle tucked under one muscular arm.

A sleeping bag.

Rowena had the door open by the time he reached it. "You can't be serious," she said.

"I'll take any room but the morgue in there."

"Sergeant, you aren't invited to spend the night." It was an outrageous thought. How could he mean to spend the night after their kiss? "I—I don't *need* you here."

"I'll bet the hell you don't," he said sardonically.

She wouldn't let him get to her. She just wouldn't. "Eliot Tyhurst and I had a pleasant, innocuous dinner. He made no mention of wanting to see me again." She threw up her hands when all Joe Scarlatti did was stand there waiting for her to let him in. "This is absurd. I assure you, Tyhurst is finished with me."

Scarlatti shook his head, every inch of him the pro now, not the hothead who'd risked kissing her. "He went around the corner after dropping you off, parked, got out and walked a few yards to where he'd have a view of your ivory tower up there. Maybe he was contemplating the stars, but I don't believe it."

"And what of it?"

"He's not finished with you yet, that's what of it. The bastard's just getting started."

5

SHE GAVE HIM a little room off the kitchen that had a studio couch with a mattress that must have been stuffed with dried sticks. Joe didn't know what the hell it was doing there because pretty soon he discovered that the musty, earthy smell that was keeping him awake emanated from a thirty-pound bag of potatoes. He was in the damned pantry! The gall of the woman! He was looking after her miserable hide and she'd stuck him in with the potatoes!

He slid himself down deep into his sleeping bag and gritted his teeth. His whole body was tense. He should be unwinding at Mario's with a couple of beers, a little chitchat with some friends, maybe a little hanky-panky with an attractive and willing woman.

Hell. He should be upstairs making love to Rowena Willow.

It was what she was afraid would happen if she gave him a room any closer to hers. He was sure of it. He'd gotten the pantry because she had responded to his kiss in the restaurant in a way that scared the hell out of her.

And him, too. Her hunger had stirred not just his body but his sense of responsibility. He had to *think* dammit, not just act. When he'd gone on leave, he'd promised himself he would use the six months to try to pull himself together. He had no business encouraging Rowena Willow to fall for an emotional wreck like himself.

Not that she would. And not that he really felt like such a wreck anymore. The fog of his soul was lifting. Was it because he was working again—or was it because of Rowena?

Two cats jumped up onto his chest and pawed his sleeping bag. He had visions of them using him for a litter box or settling in for the night, so he bounced them unceremoniously back onto the floor. Cats were all right, but not in his bed and not in this quaint little house of horrors.

Their yellow eyes shone as they looked back at him in the darkness. If he weren't a big tough cop, Joe told himself, he'd probably get the willies.

All in all he figured it'd be a long night.

IT WAS.

He awoke stiff and sore. He didn't require the usual couple of seconds to shake off sleep and remember where he was: he knew *exactly* where he was. What he needed time to remember was *why* he was there. What did a sensible cop such as himself expect to accomplish sleeping in the pantry of a weirdo like Rowena Willow? How the hell could he keep an eye on her? The house was so damned huge, an entire SWAT team could slip inside and make off with her without his knowing.

Well, he thought, staying over must have seemed like a good idea last night or he wouldn't have done it.

Then again, Joe Scarlatti was known for being impulsive. He bent rules, took risks. He acted fast when he needed to, relying on the instincts and reflexes born of training and experience. Thinking too much could get a cop into trouble.

But not thinking at all . . .

He shook off his introspective mood. It would lead him down a path he did not want to go, not this morning. Instead, he climbed out of bed, pulled on his pants and headed into the kitchen.

The only signs of Rowena Willow were the still-hot kettle and the two cats stuffing their faces at their dishes over by the door to the courtyard. Presumably they hadn't got their food out themselves.

He searched the cupboards for something resembling coffee and came up with a dozen different kinds of teas and finally, way back behind a plastic bag labeled Chamomile, a small jar of instant coffee. It took some muscle to open. There were a couple of spoonfuls of grounds caked at the bottom of the jar. He had to scrape them out. Even then, they came out in clumps that he hoped boiling water would dissolve.

An old-tasting, bad cup of coffee was preferable, he reasoned, to no coffee at all. So long as the stuff didn't poison him.

The cats finished feasting and wandered off, ignoring him.

Joe checked the front of the refrigerator, the table and the counters for a note from Ms. Rowena telling him what the hell she might be up to this morning. There wasn't one.

Guess I'm on my own. Apparently she didn't own a coffee mug, either. Then he found a freestanding cupboard holding about two dozen china cups and saucers, each one different, none of a variety that had ever worked its way into his life. He chose a design with a black-and-gold band on the rim; it looked more masculine than forget-me-nots.

"You're a sick man, Scarlatti," he muttered to himself, "to worry about such things."

He scooped out the few grounds that refused to dissolve and drank the coffee black. It wasn't as bad as some he'd had, but it wasn't good. Fortunately he wasn't hungry. He hadn't seen anything he considered suitable for a quick breakfast in his search through her cupboards. He was not about to spend the next twenty minutes cooking hand-cut oats.

Coffee in hand, he wandered down the hall to the front entry, figuring Rowena would hear him and give a yell. The morning sun was filtered through sheers on the panel windows next to the door, but instead of cheering up the place, it only made it seem lonelier. Joe peeked into the drawing room.

"Hi, guys," he said to the stuffed animals.

They just stared back at him.

He patted the suit of armor in the entry on the shoulder as if it could commiserate with his plight and sipped his coffee, trying to figure out a way to get a decent hold on the damned cup. His fingers were too thick.

Probably, he thought, he should just go home, call Hank Ryan, tell him he was out, done, *fini*, Rowena Willow could damned well handle Eliot Tyhurst herself. He wouldn't mention that he'd kissed her.

But he started up the sweeping stairs.

Sombre paintings and old photographs hung on dark Victorian wallpaper. Where the stairs curved, there was a window seat made of polished wood, no cushion, no pillows. Heavy drapes were drawn over the window above it. Even the cats wouldn't hang around there.

On the second-floor landing the doors to what rooms he could see were all shut. There were more forbidding paintings—portraits of dour men and women and eerie forest landscapes—and more dark wallpaper. Joe decided he was just as glad he'd had the pantry.

He paused and listened.

Tap-tap-tap . . .

The sound, barely audible, was coming from the third floor. He finished off his coffee in one big swallow and headed up, not skipping steps lest he trip and break his neck, but moving quickly, with a renewed sense of energy.

Rowena Willow at work.

That would be something to see.

He came to the third floor and was struck immediately by the sunlight streaming in through the bright clear glass of tall windows unfettered by drapes and sheers. The walls were painted a warm, ultrapale peach. Underfoot was a simple runner in a soft neutral color. A window seat was cushioned in a peach-flowered fabric and piled with pillows. Everything was bright, clean, simple.

Rowena, Rowena, Joe thought. *I haven't even begun to figure you out.*

Not that figuring her out was necessary to keeping Tyhurst from hurting her, he told himself. *Pull back, my man, pull back. You don't belong in her world.*

The tapping sound had stopped. Joe figured she must have heard him. He walked down the hall and turned left through an open doorway, into a large, airy, cheerful state-of-the-art office. A computer and fax machine and copier hummed, but the place smelled faintly of cinnamon; he spotted a bowl of potpourri on the edge of one of four long desks.

Rowena sat at one of them in the middle of the room, her back to him, staring at a bunch of numbers on a computer screen. Her hair was pinned up, not a strand hanging loose, and she had on a russet-colored jumpsuit and no shoes.

She did not look around at him. Joe figured she was either pretending she didn't know he was there or didn't, in fact, know he was there.

He cleared his throat.

She screamed and jumped right up off her chair, which backed out from under her. When she came down, she caught just the edge of the chair and slipped onto the floor. A thick lock of hair fell down one cheek. She was shaking. She got up on her knees and turned, holding on to the seat of her chair as her big blue eyes focused on the intruder.

Joe smiled. "Morning."

She glared at him.

"Guess I startled you."

She didn't seem too thrilled. Tucking the errant lock of hair back where it belonged, she climbed to her feet and rearranged her jumpsuit, which had gotten twisted in her tumble to the floor. Joe tried not to let his gaze linger on the soft swell of her breasts, but it was one of those things that, by the time you try not to do it, you've already done it. Rowena glared at him some more. Her cheeks, however, were flushed. Again he realized that despite her bizarre life-style and genius, Rowena Willow was not unaware of the needs of the flesh, her own included.

"I thought you would be gone by now," she said, barely recovered.

"I'm not."

"Why not?"

"Just got up. Haven't even had my morning hand-cut oats. How long you been at it?"

"Since five. I like to get an early start. I..." She licked her lips, clearly embarrassed at having jumped out of her skin. "My concentration—when I work, I'm often unaware of other . . . I don't hear things. I jump when the phone rings, a fax comes in, Mega or Byte show up." She smiled feebly. "One of the hazards of the job, I guess."

"As hazards go," Joe said, "it could be worse."

She nodded, and the flush receded, the eyes lost some of their angry embarrassment. She licked her lips again. It was about as distracting as the twisted jumpsuit had been. But then she said, "Yes, I understand you've faced a number of hazards in your career with the San Francisco police."

He frowned. "How would you know?"

With a small gesture, she indicated her computer. "I looked you up. I'm tied into a number of . . ." She paused, probably thinking of the right way to explain it to a nontechnical type. "A number of networks. I typed in 'SCARLATTI, JOE' more or less for my own peace of mind and—well, I got quite a lot."

Joe stiffened. "Such as?"

"I would think you would already know."

Joe did indeed.

"If you can spy on me, know things about me, sleep in my house, I see no reason why I shouldn't find out what I can about you." Her tone was cool but not judgmental and a nervous look had come into her big blues. "I'm sorry if it's awkward for you."

"Yeah," he said, and headed for the door.

"Where are you going?"

His jaw was clenched tight, his body tense with the pain of being reminded of why he had time to keep an eye on her. Of Matt Lee's death. Of his own role in it. He didn't bother turning around. "I'll let you know."

"If you stay—" she hesitated, then blundered on "—please don't scare me again."

He looked around at her, saw how smart and independent and yet vulnerable she was, felt a surge of something he couldn't identify—something between attraction and protectiveness—and nodded curtly, knowing he had to get the hell out of there, and fast. He had to get himself under control. He remembered last night's promise to himself: to think before he acted.

Not thinking before he acted had gotten Matt killed.

FOR ONCE in her life, the numbers on her computer screen made no sense to Rowena. They were a jumble of high-resolution dots on her color monitor. They might just as well have been baseball scores. She couldn't focus. She couldn't concentrate. Maybe she needed a break.

She pushed back her chair, blinked her eyes several times and raised her arms above her head to stretch. Tension and stiffness had penetrated her muscles; her wrists ached. She'd been at her computer for four hours straight and it was only nine in the morning.

But that wasn't anything out of the ordinary and certainly not the reason she couldn't concentrate.

Joe Scarlatti's presence in her house, however, *was* out of the ordinary.

Dammit, I won't think about him!

She clicked to the next screen of the file she was examining, hoping it would make more sense or at least jog her back into action. She was supposed to be unraveling the tangled financial network of a private winery. A prospective buyer wanted to be certain he knew all there was to know about the company from an objective—and respected—source. Namely herself.

But still she stared blankly at the screen.

Instead of seeing financial clues, she saw her tough San Francisco cop's dark, searching eyes. His rugged face. His thick thighs. Instead of thinking about the future of the mercurial wine business, she thought about the intriguing nature of Joe Scarlatti. His grit and determination. His wit and unusual sense of humor.

And his past. The last year in particular. She thought about that a lot.

A burnt-out cop.

And for her a potentially dangerous man.

Even before he'd come up to her office earlier this morning, she had known he was still in her house. She knew he was there now. She could feel his presence. He hadn't left.

Banging keys, she quickly exited the file and returned to the C-prompt.

Her hands were trembling.

"This is absurd," she said under her breath.

Before she knew what she was doing, Rowena suddenly flew to her feet and raced down the two flights of stairs, nearly running into Joe Scarlatti in her front entry. He appeared to be in a staring contest with her suit of armor. He looked around at her, but said nothing. She wondered if he knew how close she'd come to plowing into him as she had in the restaurant. Would he have caught her up in his arms again?

I have to stop this sort of thinking! We would be a disaster together!

Like her parents . . .

"We should talk," she said, hating the way her voice croaked.

"About what? You're the genius." His mood was obviously still sour over what he clearly perceived to have been an invasion of his privacy. "You must know everything there is to know about me by now."

"Only what's in public records I have access to through my computer."

A corner of his mouth twitched. "That's about everything."

"Sergeant—"

"Joe," he said. "You know that much about me, you get to call me Joe." There was no humor in his tone, none in his eyes.

Rowena was unintimidated. "So it's okay for you to know everything about me, but I'm to know nothing about you."

"I doubt I know everything about you, Rowena. I doubt anyone does. I only know what I need to know to do my job."

"A job I didn't ask you to do. Suppose I need to know about you in order to trust you?"

"Then you should have asked me."

"Would you have told me?"

He didn't hesitate. "No."

"I didn't figure you would." She backed up a step. "I'm sorry about your partner, Matt Lee. He—"

"You don't need to tell me his name. I remember."

She accepted the criticism without comment. She had no experience talking to cops who blamed themselves for their partner's death. She noticed his rigid stance, the cold pain in his eyes, and she asked softly, "He's why you're on leave of absence, isn't he?"

"And available to keep an eye out on a pretty, blue-eyed genius? Yep, he's why. Get a kick out of it, too, Matt would." But Joe Scarlatti wasn't getting a kick out of anything; his whole demeanor was without humor.

He was angry and sarcastic, but Rowena wasn't fooled—his pain was nearly palpable. "Anything else you want to tell me about myself?"

She inhaled, still not intimidated, not afraid of him. "You're angry."

He shoved his hands into his jean pockets. "Let's just say I don't appreciate your sneaking around in your computer like goddamned Big Brother."

She swallowed and made herself meet his gaze with all the courage and directness she could muster. "I can understand that. I also understand that a computer search can't give the full measure of a human being. The newspaper accounts I accessed—I'm sure they didn't tell everything. But I'm not apologizing, Sergeant. You've invaded my life. I have a right to know the background of a man who purports to want to protect me—"

"I'm not protecting you, sister. I'm using you to find out if Tyhurst is as reformed as he says he is. That's all."

Rowena chose not to respond to his nasty remark. She could see that he was definitely angry. Hurt and pained and haunted by his partner's death, but also truly annoyed that she had looked into his background without his say-so.

He raked a hand through his hair, still unruly from his night in the pantry, and she thought she saw a flash of regret in his dark eyes. He started toward the door. "I've got to get out of here, get my bearings. Tyhurst gets in touch, call me at Mario's. Number's in the book."

"Sergeant—"

He glanced around at her one final time. "Or just look it up on your computer."

BY TEATIME Rowena stood in the kitchen disgusted with herself and furious with Joe Scarlatti. She had given up an entire day to him. Not that he'd come back, not that he'd called, not that she'd spotted him on her street. She'd simply allowed him to disrupt her concentration for hours on end. Never, never had she had so much trouble zeroing in on her work without permitting anything else to intrude.

Of course, there'd never been anything quite as distracting as Sergeant Joe Scarlatti.

As she brought her tea tray up to the sunroom, she wondered if she'd driven him away by prying into his background. It wouldn't be the first time her adeptness with a computer had driven off a man. Aunt Adelaide had warned her that many men couldn't handle an intelligent, driven woman, never mind an eccentric Willow. Rowena had never pretended to be less intelligent than she was; she had never pretended that she didn't know things, didn't have a natural ability with numbers. She had always simply been herself, around men and women. And she *had* met men who were attracted to her; she'd even dated a few. But she was very, very careful about romance, and that had precious little to do with her high I.Q. It had to do with the experience of a little girl whose parents' insane love for each other had robbed her of them too young.

Scarlatti, she reminded herself, was a cop on a case. He wanted Eliot Tyhurst. As far as Scarlatti was concerned, she was just a financial whiz, and a tad strange—and nosy—at that.

Kissing her last night had been a spur of the moment thing. Because she was there and he'd wanted to make a point. Probably had been a knee-jerk reaction for him. It meant nothing. She arranged her pillows close to the windows and stared down at the street. Her heartbeat, she noticed, had quickened as if in anticipation.

"Of what?" she snorted, disgusted with herself.

Squinting, she examined each vehicle parked on the street below her just as she had before she had come face-to-face with Joe Scarlatti. She recalled her first good look at him, climbing out of his truck, stretching, irritated and impatient.

In spite of herself, she imagined what it would be like to go to bed with him. He would be an experienced lover. He would know what pleased him, what pleased a woman. Possibly he would even—

"*Stop!*"

Tea splashed onto her front, but she hardly felt its heat. She didn't finish it, but returned the tray to the kitchen, dumped the rest down the drain, and wiped her shirt. She played with Mega and Byte for a while, throwing a catnip toy down the hall toward the suit of armor. One or the other would bring it back for her to throw again, like a couple of dogs playing fetch. They were good cats—pretty, predictable, decent company.

Why now, more than ever before, did she feel the crushing silence of Aunt Adelaide's peculiar house?

The doorbell rang, startling her, although not nearly as much as when Joe Scarlatti had snuck into her office.

Checking through the side window, she saw not a tough cop, but Eliot Tyhurst, looking so deceptively correct in his conservative gray suit. She opened the door.

"Hello, Rowena. I hope I'm not disturbing you." He had a Burberry raincoat draped over his shoulders against a light but persistent drizzle; it made him look even more competent and powerful. Less of an ex-convict. "May I come in?"

"Why?" she asked, not rudely.

If he took offense it didn't register on his handsome face. "I want to make you a proposition."

What if *he* wanted to go to bed with her? She almost laughed out loud. Really, she was thinking nutty thoughts. She had better make herself another pot of tea and get herself back under control before she started thinking every man in San Francisco wanted her.

Then, as if to prove what an idiot she was turning into, Tyhurst said formally, "I want to hire you."

6

TWO DAYS AFTER Joe had stormed out of Rowena Willow's Telegraph Hill monstrosity, he sat at Mario's Bar & Grill nursing a cold beer and taking occasional bites of a black bean enchilada. The spicy sauce was enough to make his eyes tear. He accused his cousin of deliberately adding more jalapeños to his plate.

"Wished I thought of it," Mario said, wiping up after a customer, "but I didn't. You going to hang around here all day?"

"Maybe." He probably should have sat at his booth, out of Mario's immediate range, but he'd wanted some company, some distractions.

"What about Rowena Willow?" Mario asked. "Aren't you supposed to be watching her?"

"'Supposed to' implies I've got orders. I don't. Not from the department, not from her and not from you."

Mario took no notice of his cousin's surly tone. "She turned Tyhurst in."

"Yeah."

"Figure we owe her."

"*We*, Gunga Din?"

Mario grunted. "The SOB decides to come after her, somebody better be there."

"Lady can take care of herself. You've seen her. She keeps a spear in the front hall."

"You scared of her or what?"

Joe gave him a look of disgust and tried another bite of the enchilada. Hotter'n hell. He didn't believe Mario about not trying to char his esophagus. "You wouldn't serve something this hot to customers."

"Some people like their food extra-spicy. Thought you did."

"I do, but this is—do I have flames coming out of my ears?"

Mario scoffed. "Can't have a fire in a vacuum."

"Funny, funny."

"Hank Ryan called again. You going to call him back?"

"Maybe."

His cousin tossed his rag onto his shoulder with a hard snap and glared at Joe with growing impatience. His expression reminded Joe of their grandfather. The younger Mario Scarlatti was easygoing in comparison. He said, "Finish your lunch and get the hell out of here for a while. I'm sick of looking at you."

"One thing I can say, Mario, I always know where I stand with you."

But he'd already stomped back to the kitchen, muttering to himself about how *some* people tested his sense of family loyalty beyond endurance, only he had a way of putting it that was even spicier than his enchilada sauce. Not ones to cross, the Scarlattis. But Eliot Tyhurst had, and Mario, Sr. hadn't fought back. He'd just given up and died a broken man. If his grandson and namesake hadn't been able to take over the bar, he'd have had to sell it.

Joe finished off his beer and knew he'd need something more to drink if he was going to eat the last of his enchilada. Or maybe he ought to dump the damn thing down the drain and ruin Mario's plumbing for him. He was still arguing with himself when Hank Ryan wandered in.

His fellow cop was clearly annoyed. "How the hell tough is it for you to pick up the damned phone and call me?"

"Hey, Hank."

He plopped on the stool beside Joe. "You drunk?"

"Nope. Too early."

Hank scowled. "You'd be better off watching Rowena Willow and Eliot Tyhurst than wasting away in here all damned day."

"I'm not wasting away. Mario wouldn't let me. And I don't get drunk. As for Ms. Willow and Mr. Tyhurst—I don't want to have a harassment charge laid on my doorstep."

"Harassment for what? You haven't done enough."

Joe eyed him and shrugged.

Mario came out of the kitchen and pointed a thick finger at Hank. "You," he said, "get him—" he redirected the finger to Joe "—out of here."

"I'm trying," Hank said.

"Try harder," Mario said and stomped back to the kitchen.

Hank sighed. "See, Joe, you're bugging everybody. A man like you needs to be doing something, not sitting around licking his wounds."

"What would you say if I told you I've been keeping an eye on our two financial types, only I've been especially subtle about it?"

"I don't know." Hank looked dubious. "Would you be lying?"

Joe grinned, and for a second he forgot about the extra-hot enchilada sauce and took too big a bite. It burned all the way down and continued to burn in his stomach. It was a distraction, anyway, from the way he burned for Rowena Willow.

"What," Hank said, "Mario trying to kill you?" He laughed. "I knew I liked that guy. Look, I just wanted to check in, keep in touch. You know you haven't been yourself for a hell of a long time. I don't want this thing to—it's supposed to help, not hurt."

"If he's up to something—and I'm not saying he is—Tyhurst isn't going to be easy to nail this time."

"He wasn't easy last time." Hank glanced at Joe. "Think maybe he's a new man after all?"

Joe didn't hesitate. "No."

"One more thing. I'm going to be talking to a guy Tyhurst knew in prison. He says he has some information on him. He's a real lowlife himself so I'm not holding my breath. I'll let you know if anything pans out."

"Yeah."

After Hank left, Joe gave up on his enchilada and got himself a large cola and returned to his bar stool, staring out at the passersby and the milky mist. What the hell was he going to do about Rowena Willow?

Not about her, he thought. About himself and his loss of objectivity. He had worked for six months to shut down his feelings, to keep them under control, keep them from hurting anyone else. Now he couldn't stop thinking about Rowena Willow.

Then she was there beside him and for a second he thought he'd just conjured her up, but he was stone-cold sober and there was no denying her presence. The light scent of her perfume. The cool mist clinging to her hair. She had it in some kind of prim-looking twist. It was becoming, but again he found himself imagining it down, imagining his hands in it.

He sipped his soda and said nothing. Neither did she.

She wore no makeup, had on leggings and a huge San Francisco Giants shirt, and still she looked gorgeous. Her body was trim and fit and feminine, but there was something tentative about her as she shifted on the stool, twisted her hands together on the smooth surface of the bar. She seemed not so much self-conscious or awkward as just unsure of what to do, what to say, why she'd even come. She was out of her element, no buttons to push, no numbers to analyze. Joe figured she'd gotten out more in the past few days than she had in months.

Finally he said, "You want something to drink?"

She ignored his question, her black-lashed eyes narrowing on him. "You haven't been watching my place."

"You sure about that?"

He could see she wasn't. She untwisted her hands and ran her fingertips along the edge of the bar. "I wanted to talk to you."

"About what?"

"I—first I have to say I'm sorry about prying into your past. I thought I had a right."

He wished she hadn't brought it up. "Maybe you did."

It seemed enough of an answer for her. "Are you still interested in Eliot Tyhurst?"

"Depends."

"I mean, I know your interest is unofficial, that Hank Ryan put you up to watching me . . . my place in case Tyhurst tried anything. Technically you're still on leave of absence, aren't you?"

"Yes."

"So anything..." She swallowed, inhaled and started again. "If Tyhurst does anything suspicious or outright fraudulent, if anything really did happen, or does happen, I should go to the police, not to you."

Joe's entire body went rigid. "Rowena, what's going on?"

She gave an audible sigh, her dark eyebrows knitted together. Her convoluted speech, he realized, wasn't tentativeness or uncertainty or awkwardness. She was an eccentric genius who sometimes came across as a dingbat because her mind worked faster than her mouth.

"Eliot—Tyhurst—came to my house after you left the other day."

"What, does he want me to chaperon another dinner between you two?"

She frowned. Either his wit passed her by or she was deliberately ignoring it. The woman's one-track mind wasn't on a track that included kidding. "He doesn't know about you."

Joe kept quiet, not wanting to scare her off. He wanted her to talk to him. A sudden pain in his gut told him he more than wanted it; he needed it. He needed her trust.

"He wanted to talk about hiring me," she said.

"And you told him to go soak his head."

"No."

Again that deadly serious tone. Joe said, "Uh-huh. Go on."

"I told him I would meet him this morning."

This morning. "Nice of you to come to me after you let the horse out of the barn. Did you meet in a well lit, well populated location?"

"In my drawing room."

"With the dead animals looking on. Terrific. Some protection."

"I didn't think I needed protection," she said in that cool, I'm-smarter-than-you voice. Joe was beginning to think it was a cover-up, that he'd jumped to some wrong conclusions about Rowena Willow of Telegraph Hill.

"Did Tyhurst get the creeps?" he asked sarcastically.

Rowena blinked at him as if she didn't have the faintest idea what he was talking about. "Is that a joke?"

"You should have called me before you had Tyhurst to your house alone."

"I thought you might be—" she licked her lips, an immense distraction "—out on the street."

"And you not know it? My, my. I'm surprised it even occurred to you I might be able to outwit you."

Her big eyes seemed to reach for his; he could feel them drawing him toward her. "Did you?"

It pained him, but honesty was generally one of his habits and he had to shake his head. "I was here."

"I see." Her shoulders drew back slightly, as if in re-action to some kind of realization that she was on her own. It didn't seem to be an unfamiliar state of affairs. "Well, nothing happened. Fortunately for me. I sup-pose it doesn't make any difference to you whether anything happened or not." There wasn't an ounce of self-pity in her tone; she was just stating the facts. "Ex-cuse me."

She whipped to her feet, every hair in her twist stay-ing right where it was. She was a woman, Joe thought, who kept her emotions under tight rein. She *was* upset that he'd left her on her own. Only she'd never admit it, maybe not even to herself.

"You knew where to find me," Joe said quietly. "You could have called."

Her answer was a haughty toss of the head, about as phony as the uppity tone, as she marched toward the door.

He leaned back against the bar, noting what a slim behind she had. Hardly any hips at all. Nice legs. Probably would bug the hell out of her if she knew he was giving her the once-over. She'd tell him he was a worm and probably he'd have to agree.

"Rowena," he said, keeping his voice calm, no hint of the downright primitive urges he was fighting. "What does Tyhurst want to hire you to do?"

She pretended not to hear him and in two seconds flat was out the door.

Joe swore under his breath.

Mario appeared behind the bar. "Go after her, give yourself something to do and get out of my hair at the same time."

"She's trouble, Mario."

His cousin grinned. "Yeah. Way I look at it, you need some real trouble so you'll quit dwelling on trouble that's over and done with."

"Getting philosophical in your old age?"

"Out."

Joe took his advice, or followed his orders, or maybe just did what he'd have done anyway. He only knew that he was heading across the bar, through the door, and then standing in the heavy fog and persistent drizzle. He looked up the street and down, toward the waterfront.

If he were a recluse, where would he go?

Simple. Home.

ROWENA GOT as far as an ancient drugstore on the corner before she had to stop and pull herself together. She was shaking, close to hyperventilating. She couldn't see straight. Her head was spinning. She knew she'd been putting in too many hours at her computer, poring over financial newsletters and periodicals, reading every line of the *Wall Street Journal*. Trying to get her life back under *her* control.

Trying to exorcise Joe Scarlatti from her mind.

Trying not to think about her reckless plan to meet with Eliot Tyhurst again tomorrow morning.

She removed her earrings and clutched them so hard they pricked her palm. Even before Aunt Adelaide's death, she had felt alone in the world. She had learned to rely on herself. Trust herself. Now she wondered if she had just been fooling herself. Maybe she couldn't handle the real world. Couldn't survive on her own.

But you always have.

No. She had survived by cutting herself off from the so-called real world. She had isolated herself—maybe not as much as Joe Scarlatti thought, but more than other people did. Other *normal* people.

Backing out of the way of a customer going into the drugstore, she leaned against the dirty plate-glass window and felt the fog swirling all around her. She could smell the salt in the air. Exhaust fumes. She could hear the distant clanging of streetcars and the roar of a faulty engine of a passing delivery truck. She was out of her element. This was Joe Scarlatti's world, not hers.

My world is just as real as his. I have friends...

It was true. She did have friends. She did have a life. She went to movies and restaurants and took walks in the park. She was just careful about when and with whom, and about how often. Yet ever since Joe Scarlatti had penetrated her existence, she had felt more isolated and alone—as if she'd been missing out on something deep, worthwhile, necessary to her being, something her friends and clients and work couldn't provide.

Had she been missing, simply, him?

She shut her eyes and concentrated on her breathing. One breath at a time. In through the mouth, expand the diaphragm, keep the chest still, fill the lower lungs, then the upper lungs. Slowly, methodically. Exhale through the mouth to the count of ten.

One...two...three...four...

"Don't tell me you do yoga, too."

Her eyes popped open.

Joe Scarlatti scowled at her. "I could have knocked you on the head and made off with your purse."

"I'm not carrying a purse."

"Okay. I could have knocked you on the head and made off with *you*."

She managed to tell him, "I'm capable of taking care of myself."

"Never said you weren't. It's just that doing yoga breathing in public in this neighborhood—which I know and you don't—can lead to trouble."

"Stumbling around out of control would lead me into deeper trouble, I would think."

His dark eyes narrowed on her, and she immediately realized her mistake. "Why were you out of control?"

She should have risked stumbling home. She never should have stopped. "I didn't say I was."

Scarlatti looked dubious, but said nothing. His presence was making it even more difficult for her to pull herself together. His hard body, his too-knowing eyes, the mist collecting on his dark hair. He was too real.

"It seems to me, Sergeant—"

"Joe," he corrected.

"It seems to me you can say anything you want to me no matter how probing or insulting but I can say nothing to you."

He tilted back on his heels, studying her through half-closed eyes. What he was thinking, seeing, Rowena couldn't guess, didn't want to guess. Finally he said, "Point to the blonde."

"I'm more than just the color of my hair." Why, she wondered, was she being so testy?

"Okay, point to the eccentric genius of Telegraph Hill."

She didn't like that any better. She was a human being. A woman. "Don't inflict your stereotypes on me."

"And you haven't judged me based on your stereotypes of a burnt-out cop?" he asked calmly.

She sighed. "You try a person's patience, Joe Scarlatti."

"Talk to my captain," he said, grinning. "Look, let's go back to Mario's and start over. We'll both be nice. We can talk upstairs."

"What's upstairs?"

"My place."

He walked fast down the block, but Rowena, with her long legs, had no trouble keeping up. And her breathing exercises *had* helped. Or was it just Joe Scarlatti's presence—his coming after her—that had her back in sync?

Scarlatti unlocked a side entrance and led her up a flight of uncarpeted stairs badly in need of a good sweeping. Rowena, who had help with the cleaning, made no comment—not that if their positions were reversed and *her* stairs needed sweeping would Joe Scarlatti resist. He seemed to have absolutely no verbal-impulse control.

At the top of the stairs he unlocked another door, which he pushed open and motioned for Rowena to enter.

She stood on the threshold in wonder.

Henceforth, she thought, he would have nothing to say about how *she* lived.

His apartment consisted of a small living room, a galley kitchen, a small bedroom and a minuscule bathroom, all within view of the front entrance. The appliances were decades old, the furnishings spare and unremarkable, a plant dying in a window. Things were fairly tidy, though. The bed was made, the dishes were done, a tattered afghan was smoothed across the back of the couch instead of in a heap. On the other hand, an overturned orange crate, which served as a coffee table, was strewn with dog-earred paperback books, and the morning newspaper was plopped on the floor beside a scarred oak captain's chair.

"All in all," Rowena said, "I guess you don't have to worry about anything falling down on top of you in an earthquake. Everything's pretty much already down."

"Only if it were the whole damned building," Joe said, walking past her into the living room. "Mario says it can take eight on the Richter scale, but I think he was lucky the place didn't come down in the quake of 1990. You in town for that one?"

She nodded. "Aunt Adelaide was alive then. She was terrified. She remembered the 1906 earthquake, the fires, the deaths. She was only a child."

"As my grandmother would say, life isn't for the fainthearted. I'd like to hear more about this Aunt Adelaide. You want something to drink?"

She noticed the empty beer bottles lined up on the kitchen counter. There had to be a dozen. She said, "Anything nonalcoholic. And I'm not sure I want to talk about my aunt. She did her best, but she wasn't cut out to raise a child. She was an agoraphobic."

"Never left the house?"

"Almost never."

"Must have been a hell of an upbringing."

"It had its moments."

He glanced over his shoulder at her, squinted a moment as if trying to decide if she was patronizing him, but said nothing as he went into the kitchen. She remained standing in the middle of the living room, watching him pull open the old refrigerator. The door, she saw with surprise, was covered with a variety of magnets: fish, butterflies, dolphins, birds, Betty Grable in a swimsuit.

"Iced tea okay?" he asked.

"Is it herbal?"

He pulled his head out of the refrigerator and looked at her.

"A glass of water would be fine," she said. "I don't drink caffeine."

Without comment, he got out an old orange juice bottle he kept filled with water and poured a glass while Rowena remained standing, glancing around the very lived-in yet simple apartment.

Her eyes fell on a framed picture on an end table. It featured two grinning young men in San Francisco police uniforms. Both were in their early twenties. One was Japanese-American. The other was Joe Scarlatti. They looked ready to take on the world.

He materialized beside her with her glass of water. She tore her gaze from the photograph, but it was too late: Joe had followed her eyes. His mouth was a grim line. Rowena sipped her water and said quietly, "That's Matt Lee, isn't it?"

Joe sighed, his dark eyes fixed on the old photograph, his emotions hidden, buried, under rigid control. "Matt and I went through the academy together. I was married to his sister for a couple years way back when; it didn't work out. A husband and a brother who were cops—it was too much. Just as well considering what happened."

"The internal investigation of his death found you were not at fault," Rowena said softly.

"Legally, technically—no, I wasn't at fault. Morally..." He twisted open the beer he had brought with him, took a swallow. She noticed a slight tremble to his hand; otherwise there was no visible indication of the pain he must be feeling. "We were after a couple of drug dealers, real heavies. Matt was so sure they'd left town. The warehouse where they'd set up shop was empty— he was just so sure. My instincts told me he was wrong. I should have acted on them, made him listen."

"He made the decision to go into the warehouse the way he did. It was his mistake, not yours."

"We were partners. His mistakes were my mistakes. If Matt was reckless, so was I."

Rowena drank more of her water, feeling awkward, out of her element. But it wasn't just being away from home. Even if they'd been in her drawing room, Joe Scarlatti would make her feel self-conscious, intensely aware of herself. The personal agony he was trying so desperately to conceal from her stirred her emotions all the more.

"I didn't mean to get off on this subject," he said briskly, motioning toward the couch. She admired his control and resented it at the same time, wishing he could articulate his pain to her. "Have a seat, tell me about Tyhurst."

She chose the captain's chair instead.

Joe leaned over her so suddenly it almost took her breath away. "Don't want to risk getting too close, huh?"

"Sergeant—"

He held up his hand, stopping her. "Don't start. Just sit where you're comfortable and talk."

She watched him plop down on the couch, its tan plaid cover badly in need of replacement. His jeans stretched taut over the well developed muscles in his thighs. No fat fell over his belt buckle. She decided not to push him about his partner's death. She said, "First I need to know if you're still on my case."

His eyes shot up and bored through her with a heat that was primitive and very physical. Rowena felt her mouth go dry, felt the awareness rocket through her.

"Yeah," he said thickly, "I'm still on your case."

"You've kept an eye on my place?" She wished the heat would dissipate; instead, it just surged into her breasts, and lower, impossible to ignore.

"On and off. I missed Tyhurst's visit." He didn't seem too pleased about that. "If anything had happened—"

"It wouldn't have been your fault, it would have been Eliot Tyhurst's. And mine. I made the decision to let him into my house. I based that decision on the absence of any violence in his transgressions. He's a white-collar criminal, a thief. He never physically assaulted anyone." At the intense look in his eyes, Rowena felt a rush of panic. She pressed her water glass to her lips, tilted it back, sucked in the last few drops. She was burning up!

"Something wrong?" Scarlatti asked.

"No, nothing." But he knew, she could tell he knew. "I just was thirstier than I'd thought. I'm fine now. As I was saying, I take responsibility for my own actions and decisions. You can't control everything in your world, Sergeant Scarlatti. You can't make everything turn out right."

"Chaos reigns outside the castle, huh?"

She let his jibe at her house go. "Often inside the castle, too."

"What about Tyhurst?"

Getting a grip on herself, Rowena crossed her ankles and tucked them to one side the way Aunt Adelaide had taught her "proper ladies" sat. She made herself meet Scarlatti's gaze. His eyes were as dark as any she'd ever seen. What did they see? She felt raw and exposed, totally open to his penetration.

"I want to hire you," she said, hearing the hoarseness—the heavy desire—in her voice. "I want to pay you for your work on my behalf. I would feel better about it if I did."

Joe shook his head without hesitation. "I wouldn't."

"But—"

"No deal. I'm not a licensed private investigator. I'm still a member of the San Francisco police department—I can't take clients. Let's just keep this arrangement unofficial."

She frowned. "That leaves me with little control over you."

Again his gaze probed and seared and thoroughly aroused her. Was it deliberate? Did he *know* what he was doing to her? Or was it just her, her reaction to him?

"You hold that thought," he told her finally.

His voice was quiet and determined, as if he knew he had her close to melting. Before his words had fully registered, she was on her feet, striding toward the kitchen. She set her glass in the sink, wishing she could splash her face with cold water. But that would be too obvious.

Joe was behind her.

"I'm sure we're overstating Tyhurst's threat," she said crisply. "He's not out for revenge. He just wants my brain. That—that's what everyone wants from me."

"I don't."

He put his hands on her waist, his touch more gentle than she ever would have imagined possible for a man so hotheaded, so shaped by a violent world.

"Rowena."

She could feel his breath on the back of her neck; she didn't know what to do.

He said again, "Rowena," and she turned, sandwiched between his hard, taut body and the cold counter. She raised her eyes with a look of challenge, but she saw that she was too late, he had already seen, felt, sensed the longing that had her head spinning, her body aching. Now there'd be no denying it.

With one finger she touched the uncompromising line of his jaw. For her it was a bold move.

"Rowena."

It was a hoarse whisper this time, and he caught her hand up in his, placed it on his abdomen; she could feel the iron wall of muscle. She let her fingertips drift downward, over his hips, down to the hardness of his thigh. Suddenly she wanted to probe farther, to feel every inch of this mesmerizing man, but she kept her hand where it was.

He traced the outline of her lips with his thumb. "Say my name, Rowena."

Her mouth was too dry, her throat too tight from the impact of that brief touch, his closeness.

"Say it."

It wasn't an order but a plea. She started to lick her lips but touched the callused skin of his thumb instead; she almost sank to her knees. She closed her eyes and whispered, "Joe."

His mouth came down onto hers, hot, hungry, determined, his tongue outlining her lips just the way his thumb had. She heard herself moan, felt herself falling back against the counter. He pressed himself into her. Her hand was still between them and dropped lower, brushing against the hardness between his legs.

His tongue plunged deeper into her mouth, its rhythm as primitive as the heat that surged through her.

She felt bold and sexy, wanted.

He lifted her sweatshirt, his hands cool against her overheated skin, his tongue still probing, thrusting. His palms coursed up her sides and without warning covered her breasts that strained against the flimsy bra, the nipples as hard as stones. Her knees went weak.

"Do you want me to stop?" he asked, his breathing labored, tortured.

"No!"

It was out before common sense could intrude.

He raised her sweatshirt to her shoulders and gazed at her breasts and flat stomach. "You're so beautiful," he murmured, fumbling at the front clasp of her bra and freeing her breasts. She could feel the cool air and the searing heat of his gaze, and then the aching wetness of his tongue, the erotic pleasure of his teeth. She groaned wildly and pushed her hand against his hardness, stroking, telling him as words couldn't that she wanted more of him, all of him, that she was desperate to return the pleasure he was giving her.

Nothing could stop them.

Absolutely nothing.

He lifted the sweatshirt over her head. She shook her arms and let her bra drop to the floor. Her clingy leggings seemed like no cover at all. She realized that her breathing was ragged, strands of hair had loosened from their pins and combs.

He tore off his shirt, unsnapped his jeans.

"I've never..." He couldn't finish, but swept her into his arms, her breasts responding at once to the feel of his warm skin against them, the prickly feel of his chest hairs, the thrill of their near nakedness.

Taking her hand, he put it back between his legs. She could feel the tremble in her fingers. But she unzipped his jeans, took his hot, thrusting maleness into her palm. She had never felt such abandon.

He kissed her, languidly, erotically, his fingers slipping her leggings and underpants down over her hips, lower, cupping the smooth skin of her bottom. Her senses were overpowered. For a wild, panicked mo-

ment she thought she would just short-circuit, go catatonic, die before she had experienced the wild, thrilling
passion of this man.

But he said her name, whispered it gently, and she
came back, her eyes meeting his as his fingertips
reached the throbbing center between her legs. He
stroked her. She stroked him.

"I want you, Rowena."

"We need . . . I need . . ." She almost laughed. "I can
hardly talk!"

"It's okay. We don't need to talk."

"But I . . . it's been . . . I've never . . ."

"What?"

"I never thought . . . I never thought I'd lose my virginity in a cop's kitchen."

His hand went rigid and stopped. His eyes darkened.

She released him and bit her lip. "It's not a disease,
you know. I assumed you—you didn't guess?"

"No. I didn't guess."

Up went her underpants, up went her leggings. He
scooped up her bra and sweatshirt and thrust them
against her exposed breasts. He zipped up his jeans,
snapped them and grabbed his shirt.

"Joe, it's all right. I'm more than ready—"

"It's not all right. I'm sorry. I—" He raked a hand
through his hair. "Get dressed."

He took his shirt into the bedroom and shut the door.

Rowena got dressed.

Using a scratch pad and stubby pencil by the wall
phone in the kitchen, she scrawled him a note in a shaky
hand.

Tyhurst is meeting me at my house at eleven o'clock tomorrow morning. What you do is your choice. You can always hide in Aunt Adelaide's suit of armor.

R

She wondered if he would get the underlying meaning of her note. Because he hadn't rejected her. She knew that. He had exercised supreme control in an act of nobility she found frustrating but endearing—one didn't make love to a virgin on the kitchen floor.

Her knight in shining armor.

She didn't say goodbye when she left, and his bedroom door remained shut.

7

JOE ROLLED out of bed, literally, the next morning with the worst hangover he'd had in months. He lay on his back on the prickly wool rug. Hank's wife had given it to him because she thought his life was so damned pitiful.

She was right.

He placed his palms on his ears and waited for the world to stop spinning. Blood pounded behind his eyes. *Maybe I'll just lie here,* he thought, *until someone takes me out on a stretcher.*

He could hear footsteps pounding up his stairs. "Joe? Joe, you up?" his cousin Mario yelled.

Then there was a pounding on his door. And a worse pounding in his head.

Joe groaned. *"Arghh!"*

"That you, Joe?"

"Leave me alone, you damned sadist!"

His head threatened to burst. He squeezed it tighter between his palms.

Mario banged on his door once more. "You dead or what?"

Just wishing he were. He rolled onto his stomach and tried to get up on all fours, felt a wave of nausea and flopped back down like a dying salmon.

"Ah, hell," Mario grumbled, and Joe could hear the rattle of keys, the turning of the lock, the creaking of the door, Mario's heavy footsteps across his living room. He appeared in the bedroom doorway. "Naw, you ain't dead—you're still twitching."

"Funny, Mario."

"What you need is a little hair of the dog."

Joe had learned the hard way that Mario used "hair of the dog" to mean anything from an experimental drink to drain cleaner. In this case, it probably meant one of his posthangover milkshakes. He put tofu, yogurt, fruit and honey together in a blender with a lot of ice, poured the contents into a tall glass and made his victim drink up in his presence.

They were a huge incentive to stay sober.

"Go away."

"Nope. Last night while you were tying one on, you told me to come drag your miserable carcass out of bed if you didn't come down by ten in the a.m. I gave you 'til 10:02."

Ten o'clock in the morning. What the hell did Joe have to do at ten? He was on leave of absence. He didn't have to go into the station.

"You want a swift kick or ice water?"

Joe made his entire body relax and lay still. His head pulsed. His stomach churned. A kick or ice water— would he feel either?

Mario sighed, impatient. "Why don't I just drag you to the damned window and toss you out on the street by your heels?"

"Fine with me."

"Well, it's 10:10 and whatever you've got going you're going to miss if you don't drag your miserable butt up off the floor and get moving." Mario made a sound of unadulterated disgust. "What Rowena Willow sees in you I don't know. Saw her flying out of here yesterday afternoon. That why you're such a pitiful hunk of flesh this morning?"

Rowena . . .

Yesterday afternoon. In the kitchen. Soft, pink-tipped breasts. Milky skin. Wide, passion-filled blue eyes. Moans of wanting, hands of unbelievable temptation, of sweet torture.

Joe bolted up onto his knees. The blood drained out of his head too fast and for a second he thought he'd pass out, which would no doubt prompt Mario Scarlatti to opt for a swift kick. Possibly two or three.

"Rowena . . ."

Mario responded with another sigh, this one of resignation. He walked into the bedroom and put out a beefy hand. Joe accepted it and let his cousin help him to his feet.

"I'll be downstairs in five minutes," Joe said.

"You okay?"

Joe didn't dare nod. He couldn't have his head exploding when he had work to do. He just looked at his cousin and said, "Yeah. Thanks. I was waking up, but there's no telling if I'd have come to in time."

"I'll have a shake waiting."

Moving as fast as he could, Joe put on a clean shirt and pair of jeans and slipped on his running shoes, opting to tie them later. He just couldn't bend down that long. He stumbled into the bathroom, filled the washbasin with cold water and stuck his face in it. He held his breath for as long as he could, blew some bubbles and held it a few seconds longer.

"Be a hell of a thing if you drowned yourself," he muttered, examining his reflection in the cracked medicine cabinet mirror.

Bad. Real bad. Bloodshot eyes. Bags. Dark circles. Enough beard growth to look scruffy but not sexy. Breath that would wipe out entire populations.

He brushed his teeth and gargled with his least favorite, most powerful mouthwash.

"Gotta stay away from eccentric geniuses, Joe m'boy."

So what was he doing half killing himself to race to her rescue? Probably wouldn't need him. Could manage on her own, thank you very much.

Virgin that she was.

Damned knight in shining armor that he was. He could have avoided this hangover if he'd made love to her right there on the kitchen floor, just the way she'd wanted. The way *he'd* wanted.

They'd come so close.

Another two seconds and he would have been inside her. Making love to her. Trying his damnedest to let her body consume his pent-up desire for her. He would have made love to her all afternoon, all night if he'd had to.

He had a hell of a lot of pent-up desire for her. Still did.

"Arghh!"

He grabbed a towel and rubbed his face hard, then made himself tie his shoes. Better to think about his aching head than aching other parts of his body. He hadn't felt so rotten in months.

He hadn't, he thought, felt so alive.

Mario had a mud-colored shake and a thermos of coffee waiting on the bar for him. Joe knew better than to go for the coffee first. His cousin, his white butcher's apron stretched tight across his ample abdomen, watched from behind the bar until Joe had drunk every last drop.

A little hair of the dog.

"If I don't throw up now," Joe said, "I won't. Do I want to know what kind of fruit you used?"

"Didn't have any. Used a few drops of vanilla instead."

"Vanilla, huh?"

"It's ten-thirty."

"You're lucky I don't have time to kill you. You ever drink this swill yourself?"

His cousin just grinned. "Ever seen *me* with a hangover?"

Joe took the thermos to his truck and headed for Rowena Willow's house of horror on Telegraph Hill.

ROWENA LET him in. If she was embarrassed about yesterday, she gave no sign of it. If she even *remembered* yesterday, she gave no sign. Joe knew he himself still looked like hell. He could see her noticing, wondered if she could guess why he hadn't shaved, why his eyes were bloodshot, why he had a thermos of hot coffee hanging from his thumb. Wondered if she could tell that he could carry her upstairs and make love to her right now. Could even take her into the drawing room and make love to her with her beady-eyed stuffed animals looking on.

It wasn't going to go away of its own accord, this hunger he had for her. He realized that now. Like hunger for food, like a vitamin deficiency, a thirst, it wouldn't go away until it had been satisfied. He had to have her in his arms again. And even then the desire would still be there.

He gritted his teeth. Such professional thinking.

Rowena did not look like hell. She had on a sleek tropical-weight wool pantsuit in a warm, rich brown that made her skin seem even creamier, even more touchable. Her hair was pinned up, as tight and formal as she was pretending to be. The schoolmarm, the ice princess.

The untouchable virgin.

"Good morning, Sergeant," she said, her voice cool, calm, professional. But her eyes didn't linger on his, and he could see the faint color high in her cheeks, as close to a betrayal of her awareness of him as he would get. She glanced at the thick-banded watch on her slender wrist. "It's almost eleven. Mr. Tyhurst will be here at any moment. Might I suggest the drawing room?"

Joe felt himself beginning to relax. What an act. He decided to go along with it. "For him or me?"

She pursed her lips; she had a luscious, sexy mouth. "You. Mr. Tyhurst and I will conduct our meeting in the parlor across the hall." With a slight nod she indicated the room through the archway to her left; it looked friendlier than the one she had in mind for him.

He shrugged. "I won't be able to listen in."

"Do you need to?"

"Afraid I won't understand what you two are talking about?"

The lips pursed again; he saw they were highlighted with a blackberry-colored lipstick. Very appealing. He could almost taste it. She said, "That's a highly defensive remark, Sergeant."

"It wasn't a remark—it was a question."

"My point is, if I need you, I'll call." A half smile. "If I'm in any danger, you'll have no trouble hearing me."

"If I sense you're in any danger, sweetheart," he said, sexy, deliberately cocky, "you won't have a chance to yell. I'll be there first."

She tilted back on her heels, her arms folded on her breasts. "So sure of yourself, aren't you?"

"Of many things, no. Of that, yes."

And he turned on his heels and headed into the morgue.

"Hey, guys," he said cheerfully as Rowena Willow snapped the sliding pocket doors shut behind him in a huff.

Teach her to pretend he hadn't had her naked in his arms less than twenty-four hours ago.

Or was she teaching him?

He frowned and looked for somewhere to sit and have a cup of coffee. The only furnishings built to accommodate living, human rear ends were a couple of stiff-backed antique chairs. Their red-cushioned seats might have been out of a bordello from San Francisco's early, less chichi days.

A weird family, the Willows.

The doorbell rang, and Joe tensed as he listened to Rowena greet Eliot Tyhurst and usher him into the parlor. The lying bastard sounded ready to do anything she asked.

Joe hated being reduced to peeking through key-holes, but there he was on his hands and knees doing his best to see into the entry.

Nothing. They'd already gone.

He got up and paced for a full two minutes, careful not to make any noise. His audience of dead animals seemed to be mocking him. *So, Joe, does she know more about police work and the likes of Eliot Tyhurst than you do? Going to stand on your head and spit nickels if she asks you, Joe?*

"The hell with it," he growled under his breath.

He went through a single door at the back of the drawing room into a smaller sitting room of some kind—an unbelievably dreary place—and out it into the hall near the kitchen, through the kitchen, through a butler's pantry, through the dining room and into yet another short hall.

How the hell many rooms did one woman need?

And all, he noted, were as dark and forbidding and spooky as every other room he'd ventured into in the peculiar house, except for Rowena's office on the third floor. He had a sudden urge to see the tower room she'd visited every afternoon at five while he'd watched her from the street, thinking he was unseen. A mistake where eccentric geniuses were concerned, he now realized. He had been as arrogant as charged.

He came to the library and slowed, hearing voices. Hers, Tyhurst's.

His instincts and training taking over, he walked softly across the thick Persian carpet, making no sound in the darkened, eerie library. A stuffed owl watched him from a tall stand. He half expected it to spread its wings and swoop down after him, wondered what would come to Rowena's mind if Mario started talking to *her* about a little hair of the dog. Probably not milkshakes or experimental drinks.

The connecting door to the parlor was shut tight. Joe pressed his ear to it. *You're a pro,* he assured himself, *not a sneak.*

Tyhurst and Rowena were talking numbers and stuff. The ex-convict understood her jargon. They spoke each other's language.

If Tyhurst was running a new scam, Joe would need Rowena to decipher for him what the hell the two of them had talked about. But if Tyhurst was out for revenge against the woman who'd put him in prison, Joe wouldn't need anyone's help. He'd damned well know what was going on. And he'd know what to do about it.

Skewer the SOB.

"I'd like your analysis," Tyhurst was saying. Just the sound of his voice irritated Joe. "I know you have no reason to trust me—I appreciate your even agreeing to see me again. I had no right even to hope that you would go out for dinner with me, never mind entertain the prospect of taking me on as a client."

Joe made a face. *Laying it on a little thick, Tyhurst.*

Rowena didn't seem to think so. "I have no grudge against you, Eliot."

Eliot?

"Then you'll help me?"

"I can't work for you." She was using her cool, high-IQ tone. "It would be unethical on my part after having . . . given our past."

There was a short, pained silence. *Eliot* said, "I understand, but I'd like you to think over my proposition. I'm only trying to do the right thing. I will never, never repeat the mistakes I made. I know that even if no one else does."

"I'm sure people will realize that, given time."

Like hell; Joe wouldn't.

"I just want to be absolutely certain," Tyhurst went on, "that I don't tread even close to the line the authorities drew for me. You know I'm banned from certain financial activities. I don't want to touch anything that might raise suspicions, however incorrect they may be. I know in my own heart I'm reformed."

Damned con man, Joe thought. But he had to give the bastard credit; he certainly was slick. Even a small part of Joe wanted to believe him.

Tyhurst went on in that vein for a few more minutes. Apparently Rowena was supposed to do some financial analysis for him on a new venture he was undertaking and make sure he didn't cross any lines, get into anything, not just from which he was barred by law, but that would raise eyebrows. One would think the bastard would know, Joe thought.

Which was more or less what Rowena told him, except she was more polite and long-winded about it.

She'd dismissed him and as far as Joe could tell was showing him the door when Tyhurst—*Eliot*—abruptly said, "Rowena, I want to see you again."

And Joe heard it in his voice. Knew in his gut that the man had precious little interest in Rowena Willow's impressive capabilities with matters financial.

Eliot Tyhurst wanted to get her into bed. Whether as part of a revenge scheme or just because he'd been in prison for a long time and she was a beautiful woman, Joe couldn't say. But he knew.

He went rigid, ready to tear through the door—*on what grounds? And to do what?* Hell if he knew. Ring the bastard's neck. *And how are you any better? As if you haven't thought about getting her into bed yourself.*

As if he hadn't almost done it.

Hell, they'd never have even made the bed.

He shoved his hands into his pockets and forced himself to stay put.

"I'll call you after I've given your proposal some thought," Rowena said. "I don't have your number—"

"Let me call you instead."

A beat. Then, coolly, "Fine."

And he was gone.

Joe heard her mutter something under her breath that he didn't quite catch. Then she yanked apart the library's elegant pocket doors and caught him red-handed spying on her.

She glared at him, hands planted firmly on her slim hips as he rose up straight. "It's a wonder Eliot didn't hear you."

"You did? You knew I was here?"

"Of course! I heard you prowling through the downstairs working your way in here."

Somehow Joe was neither intimidated nor insulted. "That's just because you're used to this tomb. You hear every damned creak and groan—unless you're working at your computer. Tyhurst was too preoccupied gazing into your pretty blue eyes to pay any attention to a few odd noises."

"He didn't *once* look at my eyes."

"So," Joe said casually, "what did he look at?"

Her cheeks reddened. She whirled past him and the stuffed owl. "It's a wonder you've ever caught any criminals. Your incompetence and audacity must constantly get in your way."

That phony I'm-smarter-than-you tone again. Joe tilted back on his heels. "Tough to be incompetent and audacious at the same time, don't you think?"

She was at the hall door. "No, I don't, not since I've met you."

And then she was through the door.

"Hey, Rowena." His voice was calm, unperturbed, mostly because he sensed her anger had more to do with the sheer fact of his presence than his professional abilities. Having him this close got to her. He didn't think he was jumping to conclusions: he just knew.

He waited until she turned back toward him, reluctantly, angrily. Her eyes were a smoky blue. Watching him. Wanting him. *Pretend you don't notice*, he warned himself. *Stick to your job.*

"Is the bastard up to something?" Joe asked.

The breath went out of her, the anger, the frustration. "Give me an hour and I'll give you my best guess."

AFTER TWO HOURS Joe ventured up to the third floor. This time he made sure he didn't make a sound. He didn't want to give her a heart attack. He edged into the doorway.

The place was humming.

Her back to him, she tapped madly at her computer. Lights were flashing, numbers blinking, papers flying out of the fax machine, printing out on the laser printer. Magazines and financial newsletters and spreadsheets were scattered on the floor all around her. Not one hair was out of place.

Joe could feel her concentration. She was completely unaware of his presence. He was reminded of what, before Matt's death, he'd been like when he was deep into a case. Nothing could distract him. He'd given his work everything he had.

Maybe he and Rowena Willow weren't so different after all.

The thought disturbed him, told him that his attraction to her went beyond the physical, and he withdrew silently, heading back down to the kitchen with the cats. He scrounged up a muffin that looked like something a horse would just love and zapped it in the microwave, pouring a cup of coffee from Mario's thermos while he settled in and waited.

AFTER A TOTAL of four hours, Rowena stumbled down to the kitchen where Joe Scarlatti was warning Mega and Byte that he wasn't a scratching post. Bleary-eyed and stiff, she glanced at her watch and winced. "I'm sorry, I didn't realize the time. Why didn't you just leave?"

He shrugged. "Rough night. I needed a lazy day. You find out anything?"

"Nothing concrete."

His eyes clouded. "Or just nothing you think I'd understand?"

"There you go inflicting your stereotypes on me again. I don't know what you'd understand. I don't worry about that sort of thing. I just don't have enough information yet to be sure what he's up to, if anything." She rolled her shoulders a few times to loosen up the muscles. "I'm not sure exactly what he's after."

"You for starters."

"Me?"

"Yeah. Ol' Eliot's got the hots for you."

She blinked at him. He was seated at her kitchen table, right at the point where her eyes couldn't seem to focus properly. Probably it was just as well she couldn't see him clearly, given what had transpired in *his* kitchen yesterday afternoon. She made a look of distaste. "Even if that's true—and I doubt it is—it's irrelevant. Eliot Tyhurst wants my approval, I think. If he can convince me he's reformed, he can convince others. I'm not sure why that's so important to him except—" She stopped abruptly. "Why are you shaking your head?"

"Because you're wrong," Joe said.

She bristled. "Just because *you're* . . . physically attracted to me doesn't mean Eliot Tyhurst is."

Joe was watching her very closely. "When's the first time you realized I was 'physically attracted' to you?"

"When you—when we—"

He grinned. "See? You don't know. Rowena, I knew I wanted to go to bed with you the minute I laid eyes on you."

"That's not true."

"Want to make a bet?"

She refused to show her discomfort. "You're just saying that so you can win this argument. You want to prove I'm naive about men and can't be trusted to know when one's attracted to me or not." She cleared her throat. "Just because I haven't had sex with a man doesn't mean I'm naive or repressed or—or mentally ill. I consider my decision to wait until I was ready an act of independence and self-knowledge, not desperation or insecurity."

"Uh-huh," he said.

"I—I've never allowed myself to get carried away before."

"Why not?"

"It's irresponsible."

"And what made you so responsible, Rowena Willow?" he asked quietly.

She licked her lips. "My parents. They—they were very much in love, but they brought out the worst in each other. They had me when they were far too young—"

"Says who?"

"They were barely into their twenties. They did everything on impulse. Mother would make an off hand comment about wanting to take an Alaskan cruise and the next thing she knew, Father would have the tickets. Father would make an off hand comment about starting his own business and the next thing he knew,

Mother was encouraging him to quit his job. They did everything on impulse, they lived totally for the moment. They spent everything they had and died virtually penniless." She kept her gaze on Joe. "They were killed when their car ran off the road up in the Marin hills. It was pitch-dark. They didn't have a good reason for being up there. They'd just wanted to see the stars."

"And they left you alone to be raised by a weird aunt."

Rowena smiled suddenly, remembering Aunt Adelaide. "But she knew she was weird, and she tried very hard to give me a normal life. It's true, though, she only left this house a half-dozen or so times that I can remember in all the years I knew her. Anyway, she did teach me to be comfortable with myself, to know what I want and don't want."

"To be responsible," Joe said. He stretched out his muscular legs, looking very relaxed. "Then how come you were ready to jump into the sack with me the first chance you got?"

"Because I had been thinking about it for several days and had decided if the opportunity arose, I would seize it."

"Seize it you did," he said wryly.

She tossed her head back in an attempt not at haughtiness but at maintaining dignity. "You're being deliberately crude just to get me flustered. It won't work. You're operating on the assumption that I was somehow out of my head yesterday and that you're the first man who ever provided me the opportunity of a physical relationship."

"You always talk like that? Sounds like a report on a corporate takeover, not two people who got caught up in the moment and almost overdid things."

"*I* didn't get caught up in the moment—"

"Oh, no?" he said, amused.

She swallowed. "Well, I did, but as I said, I'd contemplated that moment before."

If she felt awkward and exposed, Joe Scarlatti seemed perfectly at ease with their conversation. Entertained, even. He folded his hands on his flat abdomen, watching her. "Okay, Rowena. Confess."

"What do you mean, 'confess'? I have nothing to confess. I've told you everything."

"You haven't told me when you started speculating on what we might be like in bed together."

She pursed her lips. *How* had she gotten herself into this mess? She said quickly, "Before I met you."

One of Scarlatti's thick eyebrows went up. "Before, huh? That's about impossible to top."

"It was just imagining on my part. I was anticipating what you might be like."

"Were you close?"

She nodded, her mouth dry. "Very close. But I didn't know for sure until I'd actually met you that I definitely—that you were . . ." She cleared her throat once more, a dead giveaway of the difficulty she was having with this level of intimacy. "You were as tough, arrogant and sexy as I'd imagined. It was a . . . purely a physical reaction on my part."

"I see."

She could see he had no idea if she was telling him the truth or putting him on so she could win the argument—provided she could remember what they were arguing about. Something to do with Eliot Tyhurst's supposed attraction to her. She made herself tell Joe, "I would have no regrets if we had finished what we started yesterday. I hope you ended it for your own sake, not mine."

He was on his feet, moving toward her with an efficient, masculine grace that she'd come to recognize as distinctly, uniquely Scarlatti. Yesterday's near lovemaking hadn't cooled her desire for him, she realized. It had only made her want him more. He brushed a knuckle across her jaw, then let it skim her breasts. She had removed her suit coat and could feel the immediate response of her nipples beneath the silk fabric of her blouse.

"Would you have any regrets," he said languidly, "if we finished what we started now?"

And he caught her by the wrists, holding her arms at her sides, keeping her tantalizing inches from him. He kissed her without allowing their bodies to touch. Desire ran up her spine like a hot wire. His tongue plunged between her parted lips, explored, tasted, probed with a primitive rhythm that made her moan into him with a longing deeper and more demanding than she'd thought possible. "I don't know if I'd have regrets," she answered as the kiss ended.

He pulled back. His eyes were darker than she'd ever seen them, aching with a passion she recognized in herself, but he gave a small smile of satisfaction. "I didn't think so."

But could he guess the reason? That yesterday she had wanted to make love to a sexy, thrilling man and to hell with where it led, it just didn't matter—that she had consciously decided to seize the moment. Joe Scarlatti could be her once-in-a-lifetime chance to experience a physical relationship with an exciting man who also, if only for a time, was attracted to her. It had been of no consequence if *he'd* had any regrets. She had only wanted to know the feel of a man's body—*his* body—throbbing inside her. Wanting her. Satisfying her as she'd never been satisfied.

Today she still wanted to make love to him, to have him make love to her. That hadn't changed. It couldn't. But today she also wanted to know him, to hear him laugh, to meet his friends, to talk to him about everything, not just the dangers Eliot Tyhurst might present to her and society. Maybe this emotional attraction to him had always been there, too, and she simply hadn't wanted to admit to it.

She still didn't. She still knew that she and Joe Scarlatti were the same kind of disastrous combination her parents had been. Driven to act on the moment. On impulse. On desire rather than thought, logic, facts.

But her emotions were increasingly difficult to ignore.

Was she falling in love with a burnt-out cop?

This wasn't the life she'd imagined for herself. She'd imagined she'd end up more like Aunt Adelaide than her parents.

"I—I need a cup of tea."

He raked a hand through his hair. "Yeah, I'll bet."

She stumbled toward the stove, feeling his eyes on her. "Would you care to join me?"

"You've been trapped in this mausoleum all day. Don't you want to get out of here?"

"Out?" She looked over her shoulder at him, perplexed.

"Yeah, out. Outside in the great big wide world."

"And do what?"

"Nothing. Unwind."

"That's why I was going to have a cup of tea."

He sighed. "Okay, we'll find a tea shop."

"Do you know any?"

"No."

"Then how can you propose—"

"Come on, Rowena." His voice was teasing, but without mockery. "For once in your life let your hair down."

8

THEY WALKED.

Rowena had changed into an oversize multicolored chenille sweater—it was chilly—and black leggings. The fog had receded from the hills but continued to swirl in low pockets and still completely obliterated the Golden Gate Bridge from view. She didn't mind. She liked foggy San Francisco days almost as much as the sunny ones. They were eerie, isolating, romantic. The fog seemed to make the pastel-colored buildings and the flower boxes and small gardens stand out even more, give even more pleasure than they did in the sunlight.

Or maybe she was so agreeable toward the fog because Joe Scarlatti was at her side.

He walked fast, as she did, but his powerful legs ate up pavement where she tended to glide along. In the sunlight his face seemed even more ravaged. The man needed a shave, a bath, sleep.

Or not, she thought uncomfortably. There was a roguish masculinity about him that suggested all he physically needed was to finish making love to her.

She shrugged off her discomfort. Was it so bad having Joe Scarlatti want her?

They didn't touch as they descended a steep hill into the fog. Rowena tried to picture them as hand-holding tourists. They could take a cable car and kiss under lampposts. Wander into shops—expensive and tacky alike—that catered to tourists.

But the picture didn't quite form. In both appearance and attitude, Joe Scarlatti was too much the tough, cynical cop; she too much the eccentric genius. They made too bizarre a pair. Sexual attraction was one thing. Becoming a couple was very much another.

For one thing, it took a man who would talk. Since they'd left her house, Joe hadn't said a word, just squinted his eyes against the glare of the sun and now the fog and kept walking. Rowena wondered what he was thinking. Cop thoughts? Romantic thoughts?

Or was he just plotting to get her into bed?

She almost asked him, but they'd turned a corner and he suddenly nodded to a shop topped with a pink awning. "There," he said. "Tea."

They went inside a small, attractive shop with glass counters filled with pastries, shelves lined with glass jars of coffee beans and loose-leaf teas and about a dozen small round marble-topped tables. There were stained-glass lamps, rose wallpaper, pink napkins, flowered teapots.

Rowena suddenly smiled to herself.

Joe narrowed his eyes at her. "What's so funny?"

"I was just thinking about bulls in china shops."

His eyes smiled back at her. "You saying I don't fit in here?"

"I'm saying I'm grateful that you agreed to come here with me. I know Mario's is more your style."

"Hey, I'm not a slug," he said with a grin.

They sat at a table by the window overlooking the street, and Rowena ordered Earl Grey tea and currant scones with clotted cream from a young waitress.

"Clotted cream?" Joe asked.

"It's a lot like butter—it's very soft, perfect with scones."

"I'm sure. Okay, I give in." He looked at the waitress. "Bring me coffee—black—and a scone with clotted cream. Can I get my scone without currants?"

"Sorry, no."

He gave the waitress a devastating smile. "Leave the currants in, then."

When the waitress had retreated, Rowena said, "You're quite the charmer, Sergeant. I suppose you have no trouble with women." She smiled suddenly. "Or should I say *too much* trouble?"

He laughed. "Got me figured out, do you?"

"No, I would just think you aren't...inexperienced."

"Depends what you mean by inexperienced." He stared out at the street. "Yeah, I've been around. Was married a couple years. There've been women to share a night on the town when I wanted—but not many real relationships. And my 'experience' doesn't mean I don't want what other people want." His eyes, dark and unreadable, drifted to her. "Maybe I'm just more pessimistic about getting it."

"Because of what you've seen on your job?"

"Because of who I am, Rowena. What I've seen, what I've done, what I know. I don't like reflecting on all this stuff. It's easier for me just to shut down. What I don't think about, I don't think about. Six months off the job is an eternity, though, I can tell you that."

"I can't imagine what I would do without my work," Rowena said pensively.

"You're more outgoing than I ever thought you were."

"Am I? I spend a lot of time alone—my work requires it. I certainly get out more than my reputation would suggest."

The waitress brought their pots of tea and coffee—his was white, hers pink-flowered—and their scones and two tiny pink-flowered dishes of clotted cream. Joe examined his with some skepticism. He dipped his spoon in, smelled, then sampled the creamy white delicacy. "Tastes like something between whipped cream and butter."

"Good, isn't it?"

Rowena split her scone and slathered it with the clotted cream, wanting to resume their conversation about his leave of absence and its consequences. But she could see he'd drawn the curtain on that subject and said all he'd planned to say—probably more than he'd planned. She sensed him pulling back, retreating from introspection. Despite being a man of action, Joe Scarlatti felt his own and others' pain deeply. It wouldn't be a simple matter for him to confront the consequences of his mistakes. But confront them he would.

"I have a feeling," she said, "that no one's harder on you than you are on yourself."

He looked at her. "And on what do you base this judgment?"

"It's not a judgment at all. I'm just speculating."

"I see."

Her scone was soft and fresh, lighter than her usual whole wheat, no-sugar fare—a real treat. A Mozart sonata played quietly in the background. People continuously wandered in and out of the small, popular shop. Couples, elderly tourists, students, an old man who sat in the back with a book of poetry and a pot of tea, a young woman with two small children who couldn't make up their minds over which cookie they wanted. "The one with the sprinkles...no, no, the chocolate cookies...oh, wait—wait, I want *that* one!"

Rowena shook off a sudden longing for more normalcy and companionship in her own life.

"What's wrong?" Joe asked.

"Is it so obvious or are you just that observant? I guess my marathon session at the computer is having an effect."

She wanted to leave it at that, but Joe urged her on. "What kind of an effect?"

She shrugged. "I'm usually very optimistic about my life. Satisfied. I accepted a long time ago that I'm different, that my life would have its own peculiar limits. I have no parents, no siblings, no cousins. I was raised by an elderly, eccentric aunt. I have a gift for numbers. For understanding and unraveling complex financial systems. I am who I am. I can't suddenly stop being who I am because sometimes it gets in the way of living like other people live. Aunt Adelaide taught me not to worry about things like that but to accept who I am."

"She sounds all right after all, your Aunt Adelaide."

Rowena smiled and nodded, suddenly missing the old woman who'd tried so hard. "She meant well. I might have had an easier time if she'd been more sociable, but then again I might not be as comfortable with myself. None of us can change the past."

"No," Joe said heavily.

"You can't pretend you don't know, haven't seen, the things you know and have seen on the streets."

"Yeah, I guess. How's your scone?"

He wasn't going to talk more. She didn't push him, but smiled instead; if she wanted him to accept her, she had to accept him. "It's very good. Yours?"

"Fine. I could do without the currants, though. Coffee's great." He narrowed his eyes a moment, studying her. "Takes a while for you to come down after a long day, doesn't it?"

She nodded. "That's why I usually have tea in the tower."

"Sounds ominous—'the tower.' But I know what you mean. After a long day on the streets—yeah, it takes some time to unwind. Are you still processing what you learned about Tyhurst on your computer? Coming up with new ideas?"

Tyhurst. Of course. Eliot Tyhurst, she must remember, was the reason Joe Scarlatti was in her life.

She shook her head, sipping her now-lukewarm tea. She added more hot tea from the pot. "Nothing new. Why do you care so much about Tyhurst?"

He frowned as if he didn't like her question, but he said amiably, "I have my reasons. Hank Ryan got me involved unofficially. He was at Tyhurst's trial, doesn't believe he's reformed. I guess the man's done his time and is due a chance to go straight, but if he's up to something, tries to exact a little revenge on you, I'll be there."

But Rowena sensed he wasn't telling her the complete truth and wondered why. "It's not your usual sort of case."

"Nope. I don't usually take on cases of white-collar crime. But then it's not usual for me to be on leave, either."

She drank her tea and ate her scone, wondering if the Joe Scarlatti she had met and was so attracted to, however much against her better judgment, was anything like the Joe Scarlatti his colleagues in the police department knew.

When it came time to pay, their tea and coffee and scones consumed, Rowena realized she hadn't brought a nickel with her and felt like a fool. "And you know so much about money," Joe teased, tossing a handful of bills onto the table. "Tut-tut."

Outside, the fog had receded even more, and instead of turning back up toward Telegraph Hill, they continued along the narrow streets toward the waterfront. They had no purpose, no direction. They were just walking. Rowena couldn't remember feeling so free.

"You like just walking the streets?" Joe asked.

"Yes, it's wonderful. But I have to admit it's not something I do on a regular basis."

He glanced sideways at her.

She laughed. "You're wondering if I'm just fooling you and if I ever get out at all."

"Well . . ."

"I do, Joe. Trust me. Not often, and when I do, I like to know where I'm going, when I'll be back—I suppose it's a control thing."

"But you do have friends," he said dubiously.

"Of course I have friends. Some I've never met—we communicate over the computer—but I have a few here in the city. Not tons and tons—I'm not that type. But I've been extra-busy lately—I owe people visits and phone calls."

"How lately is lately?"

"What do you mean?"

"Have you been extra-busy for a month, six months, a year?"

"I'm always busy. But the past six months have been particularly rough. I bit off more than I could reasonably chew, you could say, which means I haven't been out very much at all."

"And Tyhurst and I are distractions?"

She smiled over at him. "Big distractions."

"Do I hear a 'but' in your tone?" he asked not so much hopefully as confidently.

"Well, I don't know about Tyhurst, but you're—I suppose you're proving not as bad a distraction as I'd first envisioned."

"'Not as bad' a distraction doesn't mean I'm a welcome one." Again that bantering tone, as if he knew damned well just what kind of distraction he was. And liked it.

"Let's just say you're a *unique* distraction and leave it at that."

"If that's what you want."

"I'm enjoying myself right now, Joe. I feel a little as if I've been in a cave for the past six months and now I've ventured into the sunlight—like a bear coming out of hibernation, I guess."

He laughed. "Bad analogy. If there's one thing you don't look like, it's a bear."

She laughed, too, feeling relaxed, unworried, more open and ready to take on the world. The Joe Scarlatti effect. And why not let her guard down for a little while? What harm could come to her?

They continued along in silence. Rowena didn't feel as if Joe was leading and she was following, but more that they weren't really headed anywhere specific, just enjoying the coming of evening in their beautiful city. She couldn't remember having gone so long without any purpose in mind.

Somehow they ended up within a couple of blocks of Mario's Bar & Grill.

"We can walk on back to Telegraph Hill," Joe said, "or we can have dinner at Mario's."

"Does he . . . what kind of food does he serve?"

They had stopped on a breezy corner. Joe looked cold and tired...and so sexy, so physical and alive and real, it took Rowena's breath away.

A corner of his mouth twitched. "Not clotted cream, for sure. No tofu, either, unless you got a hangover. And no brown rice."

"Italian?"

"Sure."

She smiled and in a fun-filled gesture, hooked her arm into his. "I love Italian."

"Italian what?"

"Italian food."

"Oh."

EVEN WITH Mario's more eclectic dinner crowd, Rowena Willow stuck out. Her flushed cheeks against otherwise milky white skin. Her thick, shiny golden hair piled up on her head with pins and bronze combs. Her dazzling smile. Her wide blue fascinating—and fascinated—eyes. They set her out if not apart, said in so many ways she was from a different world than was Joe Scarlatti, old Mario's cop grandson, the reckless one, the one anchored in the real world. She could visit his world; he could visit hers. Joe thought of her cats and lonely house, the hum of her computer, her scones and tea and clotted cream. Could either of them live in the other's world?

He hadn't thought about the future in a long, long time. It felt good.

Maybe too good.

Mario had pulled up a chair to their booth in the corner and he and Rowena were having an animated discussion about Italian cuisine. Something about olive oil. Roasted peppers crept into the conversation. Wood-fired ovens. Whole-milk ricotta versus part-skim. Italian wines versus California wines. Rowena was drinking a California red wine from Sonoma Valley.

Joe sipped his beer, satisfied to catch snatches of what the two of them were talking about. To watch Rowena's mouth on the thin rim of her glass. He wasn't picky about food himself, but a woman's mouth—that was something to be a connoisseur of. He noticed the fullness of her lower lip, the way her tongue would sneak out and lick the wine off her mouth after she drank.

She was good with people, he thought. Better than he ever would have expected sitting out on her street those first days, watching her *Ivanhoe* house. He wondered if she needed to be around people more than she could let herself admit.

Finally Mario heaved himself up. It was still early for dinner and he wasn't as pressed in the kitchen, where he had help at night anyway. "I'll fix you up a nice egg-plant parmesan—light on the oil, fresh rotelli on the side, splash of red wine in the sauce. You'll love it." He glanced down at Joe. "You look a sight better than you did this morning. But next time shave before you come to dinner."

"You sound like Grandma," Joe said.

"Yeah, go see her when you look like that and she'll shave you with a butcher knife." Mario turned back to Rowena, his expression softening. "I'll fix you a nice salad, too, tossed with just a teaspoon of my special Italian dressing. How's that sound?"

She was beaming under the attention. "Wonderful."

After Mario had gone, Joe settled back in his seat and eyed Rowena. "Eggplant parmesan isn't on the menu."

"It isn't?"

"No. Mario's probably sending a busboy out to the grocery now for an eggplant."

Her cheeks colored. "Well, I never suggested—"

"You didn't have to. He likes you. First woman I've ever brought around he's done anything more than grunt at." In spite of himself, Joe was pleased. "Not that I give a damn what Cousin Mario thinks."

"He seems like a nice man," Rowena said judiciously.

Joe laughed. "You should have seen him this morning. He offered to throw me out the window feet first."

"And what did you do to deserve such a threat?"

"Who says I deserved it?"

"I can't imagine a charmer like Mario making such a threat unless it was warranted."

"You've known him half an hour!"

She sniffed. "I make quick judgments."

"Yeah, well, you may have a genius IQ but that doesn't mean you know my cousin better than I do. That snake has been on my case for six months. Runs me out of here every chance he gets." Joe grunted. "Charmer my hind end."

Rowena, he saw, was grinning, her blue eyes gleaming in the dim light of the bar. "You take me far too seriously, Joe Scarlatti. And probably your cousin Mario, too. Probably life in general. Despite your wit and sense of humor, you are at root a very serious man."

He leaned forward, his forearm pressed against the edge of the scarred pine table. "You're bluffing, Rowena Willow. You haven't come close to figuring me out. You don't know what I am at root."

She sipped her wine and said over the rim of the glass, "Don't I?"

"Dammit, woman—"

"Oh, so it's 'woman' now?" She set her glass down and tossed her head back; if her hair were down, it would have been a sexy gesture. "I rather like the way you say Rowena."

He squinted at her, intrigued by this glimpse he was getting of a looser Rowena Willow. "How much wine have you had?"

"Not much. I'm—how did you put it? Letting my hair down. Yes, that was it."

"Then let it down," he said.

"What?"

"Pull out a few pins and combs, Rowena. Let it down all the way."

"I always wear my hair up."

"Even in bed?" he asked in a husky voice.

But she was spared answering by the unexpected arrival of Hank Ryan. He did a double take on Rowena. "Whoa," he said, "didn't expect to find you here."

She graced him with a polite smile. "Hello, Sergeant Ryan. Would you care to join us?"

He slid into the booth next to Joe. "I can only stay a minute. How're things going?"

Joe couldn't tell whether the question was directed at him or at Rowena, but she answered, "Very well, thank you. So far Mr. Tyhurst has done nothing to justify your concern. You *did* twist Sergeant Scarlatti's arm so that he would keep an eye on me? I don't believe I've ever gotten a straight answer to that question."

Hank frowned. "It didn't take much twisting."

"Why not?"

"Beg pardon?"

"White-collar crime isn't his area of expertise. We'd never met. He didn't know me. And he had no personal or professional interest in taking on this case."

She was sounding like a damned detective, Joe thought, refusing to squirm.

Hank shifted in his chair, looking as if he wished he'd snuck back out once he'd seen Joe with Rowena. "He needed the work," Hank said finally. "He knew it, and I knew it."

"So." Rowena pushed her lips up, then took another swallow of wine. Joe could see her computer-mind at work. He knew he'd have to get around to telling her about his grandparents. It just wasn't an easy topic to bring up to a woman who made her living keeping people from making financial mistakes. "What you're saying is that I was a convenient excuse to try to renew Joe Scarlatti's interest in his work. You were worried about him?"

With a sideways glance at Joe that said he felt like a fly on a light bulb, Hank said, "A lot of us were worried about Joe."

"I see. And presumably you were more interested— and still are—in catching Eliot Tyhurst if he's up to no good than in actually protecting me from harm."

"Ms. Willow—"

"That wasn't a question. It requires no answer. What I'm saying," she went on icily, "is that I'm a pawn in your game to find out if Tyhurst truly has reformed and to get Joe Scarlatti back in uniform."

"He doesn't really wear a uniform, he's plain-clothes—"

Her gaze shut him up. "That's splitting hairs, Sergeant Ryan. You know perfectly well what I mean."

Joe stretched out his legs and cleared his throat. "Mind if Joe Scarlatti says a few words?"

His colleague and—what the hell *was* Rowena Willow to him? Not a client. Not even a lover. An almost lover? She didn't look much like she wanted to go to bed with him at the moment. Whatever she was, she and

Hank turned their attention to him as if just remembering he was there.

Joe said, "First of all, Tyhurst is a snake, whether we end up locking him up again or not. Second, I'm riding out the end of a six-month leave of absence and will make my own decision about what to do when the time comes. Third, if I have to protect you, Rowena, from physical harm, I will."

"I'm under no threat whatsoever of—"

He silenced her by holding up a hand and talking louder than she was. "And if Tyhurst is trying to run something on you—meaning he's pulling some kind of financial scam on you—I can't help you. In fact, I should wish the poor bastard good luck because you're smarter than he is, you can spend more time at a computer than most human beings and you'll catch him and hang him out to dry. By the time you get through with him, Tyhurst would be glad to see the police."

Hank looked more relaxed, in his element. "Think that's what he's up to, trying to suck Rowena into some kind of financial scam he's running? Get his revenge and get back into the game at the same time?"

"It's possible," Joe said. He could see that Rowena was fuming now that *she* was being referred to in the third person.

"But you don't think so," Hank said thoughtfully.

Joe shook his head. "I think he's out for revenge, straight and simple. *Physical* revenge."

Hank raised up in his seat. "Anything I can take to the captain, get a twenty-four-hour watch on her?"

"No," Rowena said sharply, "there isn't."

But Hank was looking to Joe for an answer. "She's right," he admitted. "Tyhurst hasn't made any overt threats. I'm just going on gut. I listened in on the two of them meeting this morning. He's attracted to her, wants to woo her, then..." He lifted his shoulders, trying to deny the tension he was feeling as he imagined what Tyhurst would do. But he couldn't maintain objectivity, not where Rowena was concerned. "Then he'll make his move. And he'll cover his tracks."

"What meeting?" Hank asked, his concern knitting his eyebrows together.

Joe filled him in, deliberately using police jargon that Rowena, given how much she knew about everything else, probably could translate. But it would remind her that he was a professional. He was a cop, and whatever else had erupted between them, his first and primary obligation to her—his *only* obligation, dammit—was as a cop.

And what the hell, it would tell her that he knew a few things she didn't know.

When he finished, Hank let out a long breath. "You know, the bastard could be on the up-and-up."

"Could be," Joe agreed. "But he's sounding just too clean to me. He was a model prisoner, and now he's going to be a model ex-con? I don't buy it. The SOB stole millions of dollars and lost it because of a plucky financial whiz—a fluke."

Rowena's fingers were stiff on her wineglass. "I hate that word, 'plucky.' It's so condescending. Do you ever hear a man being called plucky?"

Hank didn't seem to have heard her. "He's got to have a lot of pent-up anger toward her. I saw it seething when he was on trial. I don't buy it that he's romancing her. Just doesn't work for me."

Wanting to go to bed with her, Joe thought, and romancing her were two different things.

He winced. Was he just as bad as Eliot Tyhurst after all?

As if Hank were reading his thoughts, he said, "Going to bed with her, yeah, maybe I could swallow him wanting to do that—but only in the context of exacting revenge."

Rowena reddened. Set down her glass hard. Swept to her feet. "I'm leaving," she announced.

Joe caught her by the wrist and held her still.

Hank looked embarrassed. "No, wait, I'll leave. I'm sorry, I should have been more subtle. I didn't mean to upset you."

"I'm not upset. You have every right—every duty—to discuss Mr. Tyhurst's intentions. That doesn't bother me. I'm annoyed, however, that you pretend I'm not even here, that *my* opinion of his intentions doesn't count. I've spent more time with him than either of you." She was so mad she was shaking. "I've—I've probed his finances."

Hank raised an eyebrow and looked at Joe.

"That's tough to beat," Joe said, straight-faced.

Rowena would have thrown the rest of her wine at him if she weren't so repressed. Lord knew he deserved it. Wouldn't bother Mario, either. He'd probably applaud. But instead she satisfied herself with an ice-cold look at the two cops.

Hank pushed back his chair, contrite. "Keep me posted. I'm—you remember what we discussed the other day?"

The possible snitch, Joe thought. He remembered, and nodded.

"I'll be in touch," Hank said. He mumbled a goodbye to Rowena and beat a path to the door before she could wrest herself from Joe's hold and follow him out.

"Let me go," she said in a low voice.

"You going to run away?"

"I'm going to leave. That's not running away."

Joe loosened his grip, stroking the inside of her wrist with his thumb. He saw her bite her lower lip. So, she wasn't unaffected. But she wasn't about to sit on his lap and run her fingers through his hair, either. "What about Mario's eggplant parmesan?" he asked.

"I'm sure he knows how trying you can be."

"He'll be disappointed if you leave."

"But he would understand."

"You'd walk back to your castle by yourself?"

"I could call a cab," she said.

"And pay him with what?"

"I—" She glared at him. "I could make him wait on the curb, run inside, get some money and pay him. I have options, Sergeant, besides you."

"Sit down, Rowena. Have another glass of wine. Here, I'll flag Mario and have him bring out a basket of bread." Still holding on to her wrist, Joe got up halfway from his seat at the booth and yelled, "Hey, Mario, how 'bout some of your special garlic bread?"

Ordinarily Mario would have told him to go to hell or get it himself, but tonight Joe was with Rowena Willow and his cousin was smitten. He called from behind the bar, "Sure, coming right up."

"Never," Joe said to her, "be rude to a man who makes garlic bread with fresh garlic and real butter."

Rowena raised an eyebrow.

"It's out of this world. Beats a currant scone with clotted cream hands down."

"We'll see about that," she said, deliberately haughty, not ready to give up. But she did sit down, and Joe released her.

AFTER DINNER, they took a direct route back to Telegraph Hill. It was mostly uphill, and by the time they reached her door, Rowena's legs ached along with her mind.

Joe Scarlatti was the most enigmatic man she had ever met. More elusive than the most complicated financial network she had ever unraveled. More frustrating.

Certainly more alive. Indeed, he made *her* feel alive.

How, she wondered, did she make him feel? She knew he'd tried to shut down his feelings as a result of his partner's death. But he had too many friends, too close a family—they would keep him from closing himself up completely. Besides, he was a man who felt and felt deeply, no matter how hard he tried not to or how much he tried to deny it.

He hadn't, as Rowena had half expected, invited her upstairs to his apartment after dinner but instead had offered to walk her home. She'd retorted that she could walk herself home. He'd remarked in turn that she knew damned well what he meant and if she wanted to walk all the way back to her mausoleum by herself, then *fine*. Did she have to pick apart every damned word he said? Lord, he muttered, but she was stubborn. Besides which, he had to fetch his truck.

She'd relented, admitting to herself if not to him that she was glad for his company. It would have been a lonely walk without him.

Until meeting him, she had not thought much about being lonely. Alone, yes. But not lonely. It was a fine, but important, distinction.

He lingered on her doorstep while she fumbled for a key hidden in some exterior scrollwork. She noticed his frown in the lamplight. "What's wrong?" she asked.

"You should take your keys with you."

"Usually I do, but I didn't want to be encumbered by a handbag or hip-pack—"

"Someone could see you out here and help themselves to the place one day when you're not home." His gaze hardened. "Or when you are."

"I change my hiding place frequently."

"Doesn't matter. They know a key's hidden, they'll find it."

She shivered at his ominous words. "How unpleasant. You're dampening my optimistic view of human nature."

"I'm not a pessimist or a cynic, Rowena."

"Just a realist?"

He said, "Yeah, just a realist."

She stuck her key in the door. "I'll remember your advice. Thank you." She hesitated. "Are you going home now?"

He nodded curtly, his hands shoved deep into the pockets of the charcoal-colored sweater he'd grabbed from Mario's kitchen, his cousin griping at him about what in hell it was doing there. "Good night, Rowena," he said softly. "I enjoyed this evening."

"I did, too."

And she was inside, the door echoing as she shut it firmly behind her. She could hear Mega and Byte padding down the stairs to greet her, could hear the hissing of the old heating system as it struggled against the dropping temperature. Could hear her own ragged breathing.

Tears sprang hot in her eyes.

Joe Scarlatti had pulled back from her. He had decided that he had to be noble. Going to bed with a virgin, a woman who knew numbers and money and business, wasn't his style. He wouldn't use her and drop her.

She had never been the kind of woman men came to for short-term liaisons. For one- or two-night stands. For sex. She had always been proud of not jumping into bed just to please a man. She had decided long ago that she would rather wait until she was ready than to get involved in a physical relationship just because a man expected or demanded it of her. A man who made such demands, she'd told herself, wasn't worth the risks.

Not that many had.

But it had never occurred to her that when she was, in some unspecified, unpredictable future, ready, that the man she wanted wouldn't, in turn, want her.

But Joe Scarlatti *did* want her. She was sure of it! Then why weren't they upstairs together?

Was he trying to shove her out of his life because of his own problems? Because he didn't *want* to feel again?

She frowned, heading slowly upstairs. She would take a long bath scented with relaxing bath salts and tell herself that Joe had gone home tonight because the man was dead on his feet. She would tell herself over and over again, until finally she believed it.

JOE WAITED in the shadows just beyond the corner of Aunt Adelaide's castle and watched Eliot Tyhurst finally emerge from his car and approach Rowena's front door. She hadn't, Joe was sure, spotted Tyhurst on their way down their street. But Joe had. It had meant not inviting himself in, not even kissing her good-night. He had thought he'd seen a flash of disappointment in her big eyes, but couldn't dwell on that possibility now.

Tyhurst was ringing her doorbell.

After a full thirty seconds, Rowena still hadn't answered her door. Tyhurst rang again.

Then the door opened, and Joe's heart nearly stopped when he heard Rowena's voice. "Joe?" But she recovered quickly—he couldn't see her, but could hear her recovery, her easy confidence. "Oh, Eliot! What a nice surprise."

"Yes, I'm sure." His tone was cold, even unfriendly. Joe tensed. "I saw you with your . . . friend."

"Did you? He and I are working on a project together—simultaneously, I should say. He's an accountant."

A bloody accountant!

"His name's Joe. Would you like to come in?"

"No, I—" Uncertainty had slipped underneath his voice, as if he'd just realized he didn't have Rowena Willow all figured out after all. *Good luck, pal*, Joe thought. *You're not alone on that one.* Tyhurst went on, "I was feeling rather alone tonight and thought I'd ask you out for a drink. But if you've just come in . . ." He trailed off, leaving her to fill in the blanks.

She did. "You're right, I don't feel like going out again. But would you like to come inside? I have a bottle of wine. I'd be happy to have a drink with you."

Tyhurst was beaming. "Thanks, that'd be great. You're sure I'm not intruding?"

"Not at all. I've been thinking about your proposition. I have a few ideas I'd like to contribute."

"Another time," Tyhurst said, walking into the house of the woman who had cost him millions, his reputation and, for a while, his freedom. She had changed his life, and not for the better. "I'd like to keep this informal."

The heavy front door shut with a thud.

And Joe Scarlatti let out a string of curses that prompted a well dressed couple out walking their poodle to cross to the other side of the street. Now what the hell was he going to do?

"Whatever it takes, my friend," he muttered to himself. "Whatever it takes."

9

"IS THERE something wrong?" Eliot Tyhurst asked, sipping his glass of wine.

"No, nothing." Realizing she must seem preoccupied, Rowena forced a smile. She had not, wisely, she thought, poured herself a glass of wine. She had consumed quite enough at Mario's. "I've concentrated so hard for so many hours today that I just feel a little spacy."

"I understand."

She wondered if he did. If anyone did—if anyone could. Maybe it was asking too much.

He stood in front of the ornate rosewood fireplace in the parlor. She didn't know why she persisted in bringing him in there instead of in the more bizarre—and offputting—drawing room. Tyhurst turned back to her, his expression impossible to read. "So, you've considered my proposition."

"I've been giving it serious thought, yes."

"And have you decided, Rowena?" he asked softly, taking a step toward her. "Will you work for me?"

She hesitated. She had no intention of actually working for him—that would be improper in her view—but if she put him off too soon, he might walk out of her life for good. That had a certain appeal on the one hand. On the other she wouldn't be privy to any additional information that could lead her to understand more fully what his future plans were. He could be up to no good or he could genuinely be trying to give himself a fresh start. The idea that he was out for revenge seemed very farfetched. He'd had ample opportunity to go after her if he meant to.

She did *not* need the protection of an action-oriented cop who specialized in violent crime. So what if Joe Scarlatti had gone home? Eliot Tyhurst wasn't about to lay a hand on her.

Finally she said, "I need more information."

He frowned. "Rowena, you must realize I can't give you everything until we have an agreement. That would be too risky on my part. I trust you, but—"

"I understand," she said quickly. "I'm also concerned . . . well, it's not entirely clear to me you can afford my services so soon out of . . . after your ordeal." Her words came out in a rush, and she suddenly wished she hadn't had so much wine at dinner—and so much of Joe Scarlatti all day.

"You mean you need to know if my troubles completely cleaned me out. You need to know I'm not broke."

There was a note of self-deprecation mixed with bitterness, which seemed to Rowena directed at himself rather than at her, the woman who had brought his financial machinations to the attention of the authorities.

He let out a long exhalation. "Well, I admit I'm not as well off as I was in the past. And I know a lot of people in San Francisco think I should be on the streets, living in shelters and eating in soup kitchens. But I have some resources left." He paused just a moment. Nothing in his tone or manner indicated any animosity toward her. "I can afford to hire you."

Rowena decided to confront him directly. "Eliot, do you hold a grudge against me?"

"No, of course not." He seemed taken aback but not offended. "I thought I'd made that clear already. If I hold a grudge against anyone, Rowena, it's myself. But I'm trying to leave the past behind. It's something I can't change."

"But I'm part of your past. Why hire me? Why even return to San Francisco?"

He moved toward her, everything about him radiating confidence, sensitivity, trust. He was handsome in a classic way, one that bespoke intelligence and power; Rowena could well understand how people had believed in him. She remembered how some, even with the evidence of his abuses before them, had resisted damning him for the thief and con man he was. But she felt no sparks when she was around him, none of the wild energy and thrilling tension she experienced when Joe Scarlatti was in the room.

"San Francisco is my home," he said simply. "It's a part of me. Every day when I was in prison, I pictured its hills, the Golden Gate—" he smiled "—even the fog. It feels damned good to be back. If I have to go somewhere else to begin fresh—if I can't be accepted here— then okay, I'll do it."

"But you feel you have to try here first," she said.

"That's right. And as for you..." His smile faded, his blue eyes growing intense, and he stood just inches from her. "Rowena, I don't think of you as just a part of my past. I like to think of you as a part of my present ... and future."

"You mean on a professional basis."

"Maybe it could be more."

Rowena shook her head. "Don't. I want to believe you've changed, and I'm willing to give you a chance to prove yourself if that's what you want. But that's all I can offer. I can't let you think—"

"I understand. It's much too soon for such talk." His words were quiet and stiff, and she sensed his loneliness. He set his wineglass on a coaster. "I'd better be going. Good night, Rowena. Thank you for the wine, and the company."

"You're welcome."

She saw him to the door. Never the most sympathetic of women, Aunt Adelaide would have said the man had made his own bed; now he could lie in it. Rowena had to agree that she couldn't take charge of his life. She couldn't erase his past or take responsibility for it.

And she couldn't feign a romantic interest in him just to make him feel better.

His languid eyes searched hers for a moment as he stood on her front stoop. Then he said curtly, "We'll be in touch. Sleep well."

Rowena shut the door very firmly behind him and belatedly questioned her sense in having invited him inside to begin with. She hoped she hadn't done it to get back at Joe for beating a path home, barely saying good-night to her. But that wasn't her style. She might be eccentric, but she wasn't self-destructive. She had invited Eliot Tyhurst in because she had wanted to know more about his true reasons for having looked her up so soon after his release from prison. And because she didn't consider him a physical danger.

She took the stairs two at a time up to her tower sunroom, feeling her self-control slipping. She was out of her element with Tyhurst and Scarlatti.

Stumbling over pillows in the dark, she made her way to the windows overlooking the street and stood so close her breath fogged up a circle on the glass.

Her eyes, tired and strained, searched the dark street. She could see Eliot Tyhurst climbing into his high-priced foreign sedan, probably rented, halfway down the block. She felt neither sympathy nor revulsion, only a matter-of-fact sense of wonder at how he had changed her life: He had brought Joe Scarlatti into it.

The expensive car, the streetlights reflected in its shiny exterior, pulled out into the quiet street. Rowena continued scanning, squinting through the fog of fatigue, wine and confusion. Was this what really living did to a woman?

Suddenly she gasped. She stood very still and resisted the urge to back away from the windows. Joe's battered truck was still parked where he'd left it that morning.

Had he gone home without it? Or was he still out there somewhere in the dark? Doing what?

Rowena swallowed in a tight, dry throat. He was there. She could feel his presence. Feel his eyes on her.

Then she saw him.

Slouched against a telephone pole in the shadows across the street a few yards down from his truck. Looking so confident and sexy and masculine.

Watching her.

Automatically, instinctively, Rowena took a step back from the windows. Could he see her? Was he just looking up at her tower, but unaware she was there?

Tyhurst's car disappeared down the street. Rowena supposed Joe would be next. He must have spotted Tyhurst and delayed his departure. Now surely he would climb into his truck and head back down to Mario's Bar & Grill. Things would still be hopping there, not dead and silent as it was in the Willow house.

She watched him walk back to his truck. But he didn't climb in right away. Instead, he thumped the flat of his hand on the roof as if in impatience. With himself? Her?

You think too much, Rowena. Ask too many questions. Just go with the moment, wait and see.

He crossed the street in long strides, without looking.

Rowena flew down the stairs, was on the second-floor landing when she heard the doorbell ring. She jumped the last three steps, landing lightly. But before opening the door, she forced herself to take a moment to catch her breath and push locks of hair that had fallen from their pins back behind her ears.

Joe inhaled sharply at the sight of her. Rowena felt self-conscious, deeply aware of his eyes on her, but also strangely exhilarated. She wondered how wild-eyed she looked, how out of control, how alive. But he only said, in a tone that was curtly professional, "I figured I should spend the night."

"You saw Eliot?"

A single nod.

"He wasn't threatening in any way. I'm sure he won't be back tonight."

"Do you want to take that chance?"

She licked her lips. "It's not much of a chance. I don't believe he poses a *physical* threat to me. If he is out for revenge, it'll be in the form of trying to ruin my reputation, my livelihood, just as I did his—but he's given no indication of planning to do that. He says he's responsible for what happened to him, not me."

Joe didn't seem to be listening. He said, "Then you want me to leave?"

"No!" It was out before she could stop it. She spun around out of the doorway, heard him coming inside, shutting the door behind him. "There's a bedroom on the second floor you can use. It's more comfortable than the pantry, unless you want to remain on the first floor to watch for bogeymen."

"Rowena," he said.

"What?"

He sighed, apparently abandoning what he had intended to say. "If I'm going to stay, I need to run back to my place and pick up a few things. I'll be back in twenty, thirty minutes."

"I'll be here." She thought, *Where else would I be?*

THE BEDROOM Rowena offered Joe was almost normal.

There was a thick line, however, between almost normal and normal. Joe dropped his bag onto a hand-hooked rug featuring a huge red amaryllis and took in the ornate brass double bed, the empty Victorian bird cage on a stand in one corner, the huge, carved wardrobe. Cream-colored lace hung on the windows and covered the bed, and the wallpaper was an overpowering design of red flowers.

A little much, perhaps, but nothing too weird.

The artwork was what just about crossed the line for Joe. He nodded to a painting above the bird cage that showed a half-dozen wolves prowling through snowy woods. "What's that for, in case a guest might be prone to sweet dreams?"

Rowena seemed to notice it for the first time. "It is rather vicious-looking, isn't it?"

"Not real restful." He pointed to the portrait above the bed of a bearded, dour, beady-eyed old man in a turn-of-the-century suit. "And who's that sourpuss? Be tough to thrash around in the bedsheets with him looking on."

Rowena glanced at him quickly, then carefully cleared her throat. "That's my great-grandfather—my Aunt Adelaide's grandfather, Cedric Willow."

"Was he weird, too?"

"He made quite a lot of money in railroads. He was quite the adventurer. He hunted buffalo and ventured to Alaska, the Far East. He built this house."

Joe grunted. "Enough said."

"Aunt Adelaide was a good-hearted woman," Rowena went on, without prompting, "but she didn't have a normal upbringing. She lost her only brother, my grandfather, when she was still a little girl. He was much older, already married with a child of his own."

"That child was your father?"

She nodded. Her eyes seemed even bigger in the dim light, her cheekbones more prominent. Joe acknowledged his desire to pull the pins from her hair, to stroke it, feel its softness beneath his fingers, but he fought against the urge. He had sensed Rowena's wariness upon his return from Mario's with his overnight bag— not of him so much as of herself and her own feelings. He thought he understood.

"This was an unusual place to grow up, I now realize," she said without resentment. She accepted—if didn't approve of—her odd upbringing. "Aunt Adelaide did her best to provide me with a happy childhood. She had her quirks, and money was always a struggle because she refused to sell this place. But I'm afraid I'm a lot like him." She gestured to old Cedric.

"In what way?" Joe asked. "You sure as hell don't look like him."

She smiled. "He had a gift for remembering things as well. Not many of his contemporaries understood him, but that was all right with him. He had his friends, and even if they were few in number, they were very close. But never mind. I'm sure you're tired. There's a bathroom down the hall, second door on the left. If you need anything, just give a yell up the stairs."

"The third floor's all yours, is it?"

She glanced back over her shoulder at him, on her way to the door. "The whole house is mine, Sergeant. Good night."

He could have let her have the last word.

But he wasn't the type.

He said, "Rowena," and was behind her in two long steps, and when she spun around, she came within inches of barreling into his chest. He said again, more softly, controlling the heat surging through him, "Rowena," and touched her hair. It was as soft and silken as he had imagined. It fired not only his body but his soul. He traced her mouth with his thumb, then followed with his lips. Just his lips. He felt the shudder go through her but kept himself from deepening the kiss. He needed to show restraint—not just for her sake, but for his—when making love to Rowena Willow.

Because he would. One day very soon he would.

Now.

No. Not now.

He pulled himself away from her softness, saw the want in her eyes. He wanted more than a chaste kiss, so much more. But he heard himself say, "Good night, Rowena."

She said nothing in return. She retreated quickly, quietly, and in a few seconds Joe could hear her padding softly up to the top floor of her bizarre castle.

He checked out the bathroom down the hall. It was elegant but old-fashioned, straight out of the 1930s. Pale yellow Egyptian cotton bathsheets hung on a freestanding rack, and there was a porcelain dish of oatmeal soap. Even the woman's damned soap was made of oatmeal.

Joe got cleaned up and returned to his room.

He wasn't sleepy. Didn't feel like reading. Couldn't pace around the big drafty house in his underwear. Didn't even have a radio in his room. Damned place was quiet as a tomb. Hell, he thought, recalling the drawing room, it *was* a tomb.

He pulled back the bedcovers and lay down flat on his back on the soft, cool sheets.

Nobility was for the birds. Every fiber of his being wanted to be on the third floor with Rowena Willow.

He wanted to see her smile, hear her laugh, feel her wanting him again.

He physically ached.

His only consolation was that he was positive—beyond the realm of doubt—that she was upstairs suffering just as much as he was.

So why the hell don't you march on up there and make love to her? Because you can't. You promised yourself.

He had indeed. Rowena had to be ready. He wasn't going to let her off the hook by making the first move, capitalizing on the electricity between them. He wasn't going to create the moment for them to get carried away with. Nope. No way. Uh-uh. It was her turn.

If he just wanted to satisfy his physical desire for her, he would leap up to the third floor in a single bound. But he wasn't interested only in taking from Rowena. He wanted to give to her as well.

Give her what?

He was a burnt-out cop. He lived in a crummy two-room apartment above a bar. He blamed himself for his partner and best friend's death. He didn't know numbers, and he hated computers. All he could give Rowena Willow, he thought, was one hell of a night in bed.

Maybe that was all she wanted from him.

He stared at the ceiling and tried to imagine making love to Rowena and then walking out of her life forever.

He couldn't.

AT PRECISELY four o'clock in the morning, Rowena gave up on getting back to sleep. She had watched three o'clock and three-thirty come and go on her clock radio and couldn't stand tossing and turning another minute.

She jumped out of bed and pulled on a hotel-weight white terry cloth robe over her filmy nightgown and crept downstairs. She fought an urge to peek in on Joe, just as for the past hour she had fought images of having him in bed with her. She had more success stopping herself from turning down the hall to his room than she had had stopping the images that had her wide-awake and on her way down to the kitchen for a cup of hot herbal tea.

Mega and Byte materialized beside her as she filled the kettle. To her surprise she had dropped off to sleep without incident, the wine, excitement and exhaustion having caught up with her. But she hadn't stayed asleep. Awakening, she'd found herself incapable of getting back to sleep, only of thinking about her houseguest.

Her entire house seemed to pulsate with Joe's presence.

"Up kind of early even by your standards, aren't you?"

His rough, deep voice caught her by surprise, and she whirled around, seeing him slouched against the door frame. He wore nothing but a pair of jeans. His arms were folded on his chest, a muscular wall of muscles and dark, sexy hair. She noticed a thick scar on his lower right side, a reminder of the dangerous work he did. He didn't look relaxed, either. His dark eyes were half-closed, watching her; his hair was tousled, as if he'd run his hands through it in frustration too many times.

How could she have fallen for a man so unpredictable and earthy?

But she had.

"Yes," she said, annoyed at how her voice cracked, "I am up a bit earlier than usual. Did I wake you?"

"No."

She didn't think she had. "Would you like a cup of tea?"

"No, thanks."

His tone didn't change. It sounded as if someone had dragged his vocal cords through sand.

Rowena's eyes drifted down to his bare feet. "I have hot water for coffee."

"Too early."

"Sergeant—"

"It's Joe. At four o'clock in the morning, Rowena, it's Joe." His eyes held hers. "Say it."

She swallowed. "Joe."

A smile softened his hard features, instantly relaxed her. "It's an easy name, isn't it?"

"Yes. Not like Rowena."

"Rowena's a pretty name—different." He straightened and glanced around the kitchen. "Kind of chilly down here, isn't it?"

"I was thinking about having tea upstairs in my sunroom."

"Mind if I tag along?"

Her hesitation only lasted a moment. She wondered if he even noticed. "Of course not."

She fixed her tea tray, using her big white porcelain teapot and two plain white cups and saucers, the only two she had that matched, and brought it upstairs. Joe followed. Rowena could hear his footsteps echoing in the stairwell. Her own hardly made a sound.

Neither spoke.

Finally, as they approached the third floor in the murky darkness, Joe murmured, "We could use some creepy music, don't you think?"

A week ago she would have been highly offended at such a remark. She would have gone on the defensive. Now she smiled to herself at Joe's wry tone. One couldn't take oneself too seriously with him around.

"A big tough cop like you," she said, "scared of an atmospheric house."

"Atmospheric, huh?"

"Yes."

They came to the landing, and she led them down the twisting hall and up the narrow stairs into her tower sunroom. It wasn't quite light enough yet that they could do without the overhead, and she flipped it on as Joe walked past her, in among the pillows.

"My, my," he said.

"The pillows are my doing." She set the tea tray on the floor near the side wall. "This room was much like the other rooms in the house—even worse—when Aunt Adelaide died. I got rid of the furniture and replaced it with pillows."

"Why pillows?"

She shrugged. "They're fun. I collect them."

"Something to do, I guess."

But she could see from his expression that he thought her room, her pillows, were just as weird as the drawing room display of her great-grandfather's taxidermy collection. Just weird in a different way.

"I had only myself to consider. I could do whatever struck my fancy. My friends never come up here. I wanted something comfortable and informal—totally different from the rest of the house. I didn't want any furniture, any machines, nothing to come between me and the view." She looked out at the nightlit skyline. "Beautiful, isn't it? Sometimes it feels like I'm floating over the city."

Joe moved beside her. "I can understand now how you managed to spot me."

"The ever-practical Joe Scarlatti. You know, you do stand out in this neighborhood."

"I guess so."

She plopped a fat tapestry pillow against the wall and sat down with her knees drawn up. Joe remained on his feet. She poured the tea. Her hand, she noticed, had a slight tremble. She blamed lack of sleep.

But Joe could have stopped in his room and put on a damned shirt.

From his narrowed eyes she guessed that he'd noticed her trembling hands, her sudden awkwardness. He was a man trained and conditioned to notice everything about his immediate surroundings. He was anchored in the present. In contrast, an hour could pass in which Rowena would be totally unaware of her surroundings.

"You're sure you don't want some tea?" she asked.

"Why not? I'll have it with milk and sugar since I don't usually drink the stuff."

She handed him a cup and saucer, his fingertips brushing hers as he took it. The tea was hot and slightly strong, just what she needed just before dawn with a shirtless man in her tower sunroom.

"I used to play up here as a little girl. I think I read *Little Women* and *Anne of Green Gables* a half-dozen times each in Aunt Adelaide's horrid old chaise lounge. Sometimes I liked to dream I was a princess."

Joe turned from the window and looked down at her. "A handsome prince would scale the walls to your tower?"

"Mmm."

She met his gaze. He wasn't handsome. He wasn't a prince. He hadn't forced his way to her tower. There were no dragons to slay, no witches to outwit, no evil stepmothers to undo. He had asked if he could come up and she had said yes.

"What do you want now, Rowena?" he asked. His voice had lost its teasing quality; there was an edge to it that hadn't been there before.

"What other people want . . ."

"I mean *now*, at this moment. What do you want?"

She didn't answer right away.

He turned his back to her and stared out at San Francisco as if to give her space to think. But instead she noticed the jagged scar just above the waistband of his jeans, the breadth of his back, the taut muscles, the narrow hips. Instead she wondered how fast he could run and how high he could jump and how far he would go to keep her from harm.

She would go a long, long way, she thought suddenly, to banish the pain from his eyes, to keep him from hurting.

But she knew what she wanted. Right now, at this moment. She knew. And she was willing to admit it. She said, "I want to finish what we started yesterday in your kitchen."

10

"AND WHAT was it we started?"

Joe hadn't turned from the windows. Rowena felt her mouth go dry. She set her cup and saucer back on the tray; tea sloshed out onto a delicate paper napkin. He hadn't touched her and already she was responding to him. She saw the rigidness of the muscles in his arms and knew he was holding himself under tight control. He also was not oblivious to their being alone together just before dawn, to the simple fact of their physical attraction to each other.

It seemed almost easier, Rowena thought, to comprehend a handsome prince wanting her than this cop who had seen too much of the dark side of human nature.

But she took the plunge.

She said, "We started to make love. That's what I want. Here. In this tower room. *Now*."

"In spite of where it could lead you?"

"Because of where it could lead *us*. I'm not worried. We'll take the proper physical precautions and let what comes tomorrow come."

"That's not your usual way," Joe said, without condemnation, simply stating the obvious.

"No, it's not."

Joe turned around. Then, very deliberately, she tugged pins and combs from her hair, one after the other, quickly and expertly, dropping them on the floor.

He never took his eyes from her.

Long, thick, shiny locks tumbled down her back.

There, she thought, *I've let my hair down.*

"I'm not caught up in the impulse of the moment, Joe, and I'm not planning for the next century, either. But you asked what I want, and I've answered you."

Joe's response wasn't what she expected.

He exhaled heavily and took three strides toward the door. She thought for sure he was gone. Common sense had returned. Whatever it was that kept pushing him away from her had prevailed. She would remain untouched. Maybe even untouchable.

But he stopped at the door and looked back at her. He raked her with his eyes. She felt exposed, more than just physically naked. Her breasts strained against the silken fabric of her nightgown. She was hot inside the robe, intensely aware of the few inches of leg it didn't cover, even of her bare toes.

"Pull the drapes," he said.

In a moment the lights of San Francisco were obliterated and it was just the two of them in the small room, amongst the pillows. Rowena didn't hesitate as she turned from the windows. Joe's eyes were still on her.

Without blushing, she let her robe drop to her feet. Then she pulled the spaghetti straps of her gown over her shoulders and let it, too, fall.

He gazed at her for a long time, not moving from the doorway.

"Joe," she whispered, "come to me."

He was there in an instant. She didn't think she'd seen him move. He swept her up into his arms, murmuring things she couldn't make out but understood in the deepest part of her being. He laid her down on her sea of pillows and kissed her. It was a long, sweet, aching kiss that told her how much he wanted her, how easily he could fall in love with her. His passion and emotion left her delirious with desire.

But she didn't touch him. She started to, but he said, "Let me love you first . . ."

He started with her throat, touching her only with his lips and tongue. She felt the rest of her aching for their heat. He moved lower. He tasted the soft flesh of her breast, the pebble-hardness of her nipples. She balled her hands into fists at her sides so that she wouldn't grab hold of him. He moved lower, down the flat muscles of her abdomen, over her hips, licking and tasting, leaving in his wake a trail of fire.

At last he came to the smoothness of her inner thighs.

"I don't know what to do," Rowena murmured, quaking. "I want you so much."

"You've done your thinking. Don't think anymore. Just do what your body wants you to do." His voice was ragged with his own longing. "Show me what you want."

She wanted his lips and tongue to do to the hot center of her what they'd done to her breasts, her stomach, her thighs. She wanted that blazing heat *there*. Then it was. She hadn't even realized she'd opened her legs. Her hands flew out to her sides and clenched two small pillows as the heat mounted. It didn't stop. She'd expected it to stop. How could it not stop? But every time she thought she had the heat under control, he would reclaim it.

She stopped thinking. There was no controlling this heat, this man. She gave herself up to it, and it remained, consuming her, even when he drew back long enough to discard his jeans. He came back to her all hard and naked and thoroughly, thoroughly male, and there was no hesitation on her part. He joined their bodies with a single, sweeping thrust that made her cry out with a sweet blending of pain and joy and physical pleasure that she'd never known. He cried out her name, and the heat overtook them both.

When they fell apart, exhausted and spent, Rowena felt not even the faintest hint of embarrassment. She ran one hand up the hard length of his hip. "One day I want to do to you what you just did to me."

His smile reached the dark depths of his eyes. "Do you have that kind of self-control?"

She remembered how he had never touched her with anything but his lips and tongue. "You'll just have to wait and find out."

But he didn't have to wait long. Before sunup he found out just how much self-control she had . . . and, in a different way, how much he had.

Later they opened the drapes and showered and changed.

It was a new day.

HANK RYAN STUDIED Joe from the other side of his booth at Mario's Bar & Grill. "What's eating you?"

"Nothing's eating me." But Joe could hear the impatience in his own voice.

"Something is," Hank said, unruffled by his friend's foul mood. "Is having something to do getting to you or is it Rowena Willow?"

"It's your imagination."

Joe wondered at his own gruffness. What was wrong with him? He had started his day making love to a beautiful woman. An enigmatic woman. A woman he suddenly couldn't imagine not having in his life.

Still, it was one thing to make love to Rowena Willow. It was quite another to fall in love with her. And he was afraid that was just what was happening.

He drank some of the beer Mario had reluctantly brought him. *Was* that what was happening—had he fallen for Rowena? Even the question made him shift in his seat. Falling for Rowena Willow could be damned dangerous. Not for him. He didn't give a damn about himself. For Rowena. How the hell could she imagine what his life was really like? How could he dare feel so damned alive with her in his arms?

"Scarlatti?"

He sighed. "I'm still the same man I was before I got mixed up with Rowena Willow."

But it wasn't true, and he knew it.

So did Hank. "You two have something going," his friend said. It wasn't a question.

Joe just scowled at him. Mario had said much the same thing when Joe had stumbled in two hours earlier. Must have something printed on his forehead.

"You're crazy, you know that?" Hank was shaking his head in despair. "You two have nothing in common. Nothing."

"We're survivors, Hank, each in our own way. I didn't see that at first. I just saw her as a weirdo who memorized license plate numbers. But I see it now."

"You're a cop, Joe. You're on a job—"

"Unofficially."

"What you're doing is unethical."

"What am I doing, Hank?"

Hank pointed a finger at him. "You're sleeping with her."

Only once, Joe thought. Only once. Well, twice if he counted how many times they'd made love. But it was only one . . . well, event, he thought. Just that predawn collapse of his common sense.

And arousal of all his other senses.

"Hell," he said under his breath.

"Don't lose your edge, Scarlatti." Hank had leaned forward over the table, his expression turning professional. "Just because Tyhurst hasn't made his move yet doesn't mean he won't. I've got news. It's not good."

Joe's cop-instincts immediately clicked into gear. "Your snitch?"

Hank nodded, without pleasure or satisfaction. "He checks out. He had access to Tyhurst in prison. Says our boy Eliot is a cold-blooded bastard who's out for just one thing—to see Rowena Willow suffer. He's out for revenge. Period."

Joe felt a stab of cold in the small of his back. He clenched his beer bottle in one hand but took no drink. "You believe this snitch?"

"I don't know. He wants to ingratiate himself, see what's in it for him. I wouldn't be surprised if he's telling us what he thinks we want to hear."

"What's his story?"

"He says Tyhurst kept track of Rowena's goings-on while he was in prison. He didn't actually tell anyone he was planning revenge, but our fellow says it was obvious he wanted to make someone pay for his downfall and that someone is Rowena Willow."

"You have enough, Hank. Put someone on her."

He shook his head. "No evidence. Tyhurst hasn't made any threats. No one else says he's out for revenge. Our tattletale doesn't have a good track record."

"Then Tyhurst could be what he says he is—a man who wants a fresh start."

"That's right."

"But you don't think so."

Hank didn't respond right away. "No," he said finally, "I don't think so."

"I don't, either."

"Stay sharp." Hank climbed heavily to his feet. "I trust you, Scarlatti. Just be sure you trust yourself before you put Rowena Willow's life in your hands."

ELIOT TYHURST came to Rowena's house while Joe was out for the afternoon, having left a perfunctory note on her refrigerator. She immediately suspected Tyhurst's presence, and Joe's absence wasn't a coincidence, something the former banker confirmed. "I saw your boyfriend leave," he told her tightly on her front stoop.

"My what?"

He gave a small shake of the head, as if indulging a recalcitrant toddler. "I know who he is and what he is, Rowena."

"And obviously you've jumped to some unkind conclusion," she said coolly.

"He's a San Francisco cop, a detective sergeant. He's on leave of absence from the department over the death of his partner. He's a real head case. He has a short fuse, he thinks everyone in the world is a criminal. He's a cynic."

She had to remember that Eliot Tyhurst was not a man to underestimate. "Look, Eliot—"

"He'll do anything to get what he wants. He risked the life of his partner and best friend to arrest some two-bit drug dealers." Tyhurst breathed out slowly, his tension visibly easing. He opened his hands from the fists he had them clenched into. His tone softened. "And he's done his damnedest to get an isolated, brilliant and beautiful woman to fall for him. Another feather in his cap, I suppose. A notch on his gun, whatever. I can't say I know how such a man really thinks."

Rowena suppressed an urge to slam the door in his face and run upstairs to her office, bury herself in her work. She said stiffly, "Unkind conclusions indeed. And fairly extraordinary ones, Eliot."

"Extraordinary perhaps, but I don't think unkind, and I don't think incorrect." His eyes narrowed, but he looked more frightened than intimidating. Rowena noticed that he had cut himself shaving, that his tie was poorly knotted. "The truth is, Joe Scarlatti is after me. He wants me back in prison and he'll do anything to get me there."

"What makes you think that?"

"I'm not stupid, Rowena." He sounded almost sad.

"No, you're not. But the truth is something a bit different from what you apparently think." She debated inviting him inside, then quickly decided against it. His state of mind was just too volatile. "I haven't told you this sooner because I don't believe it's been my place to do so. However, since you've seen Sergeant Scarlatti and have your own ideas about why he was here, I see no reason not to tell you. A friend of his on the force—Sergeant Hank Ryan, remember him?"

Eliot Tyhurst nodded without interrupting.

"He put Scarlatti up to watching here unofficially in case you decided to come after me for purposes of revenge. Ryan wanted him to get back to work. He was afraid Sergeant Scarlatti was sliding into some kind of funk, that he wouldn't return to the force when his leave of absence ended." She swallowed. It was strange referring to a man she had made love to just hours ago in so clinical a fashion. "I'm afraid I don't know all the details."

"No," Tyhurst said coldly, unmoved by her explanation, "you clearly don't."

She blinked at him, waiting for him to continue, trying not to acknowledge her growing uneasiness that he just might be right.

"Rowena, Joe Scarlatti has a *personal* vendetta against me."

He sounded confident. Certain of the veracity of his statement. Rowena shivered not with cold—it was a warm, sunny November afternoon—but with the uncomfortable thought that Eliot Tyhurst might know something about Joe Scarlatti that she didn't know.

There was a lot about Joe Scarlatti, she thought, that she didn't know.

"But why would he?" she asked. "He doesn't know you."

Tyhurst smirked. "I see he hasn't told you."

Rowena began to shake. "Told me what?"

"Come to my hotel tonight. Without him. Have dinner with me." He stepped forward, his eyes pleading, filled with anguish. "I'll tell you more about why I need you, Rowena."

There was an obvious double meaning to his words. She bit down on her lower lip and cleared her throat, no longer certain of what she should be thinking or even feeling. She said, "I can't . . ."

"Please. Just have dinner. I'll tell you everything. Then you can decide what you want to do."

"I—I don't want you to pick me up. I'll meet you."

"All right. My hotel's restaurant is very good." He smiled sadly. "And it's generally crowded. You don't have to worry about that."

"Don't assume I don't believe you've reformed. It's not my place to judge you."

"But you've been hanging around with Joe Scarlatti. Falling for him, I daresay. His cynicism has washed off onto you. He's convinced you I can't change."

She stiffened at his accusation. "I said I'm willing to give you a chance."

Some of the tension seemed to go out of his body. "Seven o'clock, then?"

"I'll be there."

JOE CAUGHT UP with Eliot Tyhurst in the bar of the downtown hotel where he was staying, a tidbit provided by Hank Ryan. It was time, Joe had decided, for him and the ex-con to have a few words.

"Your average bank robber fresh out of prison couldn't afford a place like this," he said, taking in the elegant lobby with an exaggerated sweeping glance.

Tyhurst gave him a supercilious look. "I'm not an average bank robber, Sergeant."

"So you know who I am. Figured as much. No, you're well above average. You stole millions instead of a few grand. But you got caught."

"And I served my time. This is harassment."

"Nope. This is fair warning. I'm rattling your cage, Eliot. You're out for revenge. Rowena Willow ruined you and you're going to make her pay. I don't know how and I don't know when you plan to make your move, but I promise you, I'll be there."

Tyhurst shook his head. Joe had to admire the guy's control. "I've done nothing."

"Go on your way, Tyhurst. Leave Rowena alone. Get out of her life and stay out."

"For your sake?"

"For yours. I'm watching you."

"And I'm watching you." Tyhurst spoke through his teeth, the only indication he gave that Joe had gotten to him at all. Otherwise he looked like an honest banker out for a drink after a long day. "One wrong step, Sergeant Scarlatti, and I'll see you removed from the force."

Joe shrugged. "That doesn't worry me, you know."

"I suppose it wouldn't." His nostrils flared as if he smelled something bad. "Your only worry these days is Rowena Willow. Well, she has nothing to fear from me. I suggest," he went on arrogantly, "that she has far more to fear from you, Sergeant Scarlatti."

It was a fair point, Joe thought. The bastard just might be right. But he didn't budge. "Watch yourself, Tyhurst."

Tyhurst responded with a downright disdainful smile. "I intend to. Good evening to you, Sergeant."

WHEN ROWENA ripped open her front door for him, Joe immediately noticed two things. One, her hair was down. Tangled and shining and unbelievably gorgeous.

Two, she was ripsnorting mad. At least by her standards. She wasn't the type to kick and scream and throw things, but when she saw him, she whirled around in the entry, hair flying, and marched back and forth in front of her auntie's medieval suit of armor.

"Going to borrow our pal's spear here and run me through?"

She cut her eyes, gleaming and mad, around at him. "It's a thought."

"I had that feeling. What's up? Am I late?"

"*Late?* Late for what?" She seemed to have no idea that he'd said the first thing that had popped into his head just to get her to open up. It wasn't a question meant to be dissected. "You left a note saying that you were going out and would be back later. How could you possibly be late if you gave no specific time of return?"

"Not the possessive type, I see."

She scowled at him. "Don't try to soften me with your sarcastic wit, Sergeant Scarlatti. I'm very annoyed with you."

Very annoyed? A comment worthy of inciting his sarcastic wit, but Joe resisted. The woman was angry and didn't deserve to have him patronize her. "Rowena," he said seriously, "do you want to talk?"

She nodded stiffly, unmollified, and gestured toward the drawing room, a sure sign that she was in a truly foul mood. Joe went in and stood next to the curio cabinet of dead birds. Rowena's footsteps clicked on the shiny hardwood floor, then grew muffled as she marched across the thick Persian carpet. She was dressed casually in leggings and an oversize top, but her natural elegance shone through. Joe remembered his fingers in her hair, remembered it splayed across his chest.

"Okay," he said. He could see that she wanted herself to do the talking and him the listening. At least for starters. "Tell me what's wrong."

She had her back to him as she gazed either out the window or at the buffalo's head, Joe couldn't tell which. Maybe she was thinking about what *his* head would look like mounted on her wall.

What had he done?

You made love to her, my friend. You took her virginity.

Then she said, "Your grandparents, Mario and Sofia Scarlatti, lost their life savings as a result of Eliot Tyhurst's financial machinations."

Hell, he thought. So she'd found out on her own. He'd always known she could do it. She'd unraveled

Eliot Tyhurst's little scheme, hadn't she? But he hadn't thought she would find out about his grandparents, at least not before he got around to swallowing his pride and telling her his own connection to their pal the ex-con.

"I guess it won't do any good to say I was planning to tell you," he said.

She didn't turn around. "You should have told me the day you met me."

"Maybe. My grandfather was a proud man, and he made a mistake. I didn't want you thinking less of him for it."

Her eyes didn't soften. "You should never even have taken on this case. Sergeant Ryan never should have asked you."

"Why?"

She whirled around at him. "Because you're biased! You have an agenda. *You* want revenge."

"Rowena—"

"I thought you were objective. I thought you were a professional. I believed your advice was uncolored by personal motives."

"Rowena—"

"I *trusted* you!"

"Rowena, what happened to my grandparents and how I feel about Tyhurst has nothing to do with us." Not that she'd said it had, but he was taking a wild stab it had crossed her mind and was one reason she was so mad. "You're right. I should have told you sooner."

"The day we met, Scarlatti. The damned day we met you should have told me."

"Well, I could argue that I wasn't planning on making love to you the day we met. Not that the thought didn't cross my mind. The point is, I owed you the full story and I should have given it to you before now. I just didn't feel it was my place to expose my grandparents' financial mistakes to someone like you."

It wasn't the right thing to say. "And just what is 'someone like me'?"

"You're hard on people who die broke, Rowena."

She drew in a deep breath, stalked past him, said, "You're a snake," and kept on going.

A woman who spoke her mind, Rowena Willow was.

Joe accepted that she had a right to be angry. He accepted that he had been a moron for not having told a woman with a computer-mind like hers much, much sooner that his grandparents had been among Tyhurst's victims. She was bound to figure it out all by herself.

How had she figured it out? Tyhurst had had hundreds of anonymous, innocent victims like Mario and Sofia Scarlatti.

Joe went into the entry and yelled upstairs, "Tyhurst tip you off?" A door clicked shut somewhere in the upper stories of the cavernous house. Rowena wasn't the door-slamming type, either.

He turned to the suit of armor. "Tyhurst tipped her off."

One point to the ex-con. Joe sighed. Then it occurred to him that he wasn't particularly bothered by Rowena's anger. He regretted his role in it. He hated seeing her feel bad. But he wasn't *bothered*. He didn't feel defensive or hurt or angry.

He wasn't bothered, he thought, because he knew, deep down, that this was just the first time he had really and truly pissed her off. There would be more times. And times when she would really and truly piss *him* off.

"Ah, hell," he muttered.

All the woman needed now was to have him falling in love with her.

11

BY THE TIME she reached Eliot Tyhurst's hotel, Rowena felt wrung out. She was drained of any anger. She doubted she'd ever gotten so mad at anyone in her entire life. Joe Scarlatti had a way of getting to her.

His words kept ringing in her ears. *Was* she hard on people who died broke? She prided herself on not judging the financial mistakes of others. She'd made her own, although none as disastrous as her parents', and she'd never been so stubborn about money as Aunt Adelaide.

But they'd died broke, her parents and Aunt Adelaide. In trying not to repeat their mistakes, had she judged them too harshly?

Tyhurst was waiting for her in the lobby. He was handsomely dressed in an elegant evening suit and greeted her warmly, murmuring something complimentary about her appearance. She couldn't quite make out all the words. She'd put her hair back up into a severe twist and had on very little makeup, and a flowing, comfortable dress in a fabric two shades darker than her hair. She imagined herself out on the town with Joe. He wouldn't wear a suit anything like the former banker's. Yet he would go anywhere, feel at ease anywhere. He put on absolutely no airs.

But he had lied to her. How could she stand here imagining ever again doing anything with him?

It hadn't been an outright lie, she reminded herself. It had been an omission of an important fact.

Wasn't that worse?

He had been in the kitchen playing with Mega and Byte when she'd left. Aunt Adelaide's training had gotten the better of her and she'd said a tight goodbye.

He'd told her to have a good time. That was it: have a good time. Nothing more.

What did she expect?

"Rowena, is everything all right?" Tyhurst touched her shoulder with apparent concern. "You look a bit tired."

She attempted a smile. "I'm fine. It's just been a long day."

They entered the quiet dining room, where Tyhurst had reserved a table in a dimly lit corner. Rowena immediately ordered a bottle of mineral water with a twist of lime. Her throat was dry from nervousness and now-spent anger. Maybe she should have let loose and yelled at Joe instead of controlling herself as she had.

Tyhurst ordered scotch and watched her from across the table.

"You don't have to tell me about Joe Scarlatti's grandparents," she said abruptly. "I know."

"He didn't tell you," Tyhurst said knowingly.

His unexpected insight grated on her already-raw nerves. She hadn't had enough sleep. Her routines were shattered. She had made love last night for the first time in her life. That was plenty for anyone to tackle without having to face a man whom she had helped send to prison.

"No," she said, "he didn't tell me. I did some research on my own."

"You and your computer." He laughed.

Rowena couldn't come up with an answering smile. Indeed, her and her computer. "Mario Scarlatti died two years ago."

Tyhurst's eyes clouded; she couldn't read his expression. "I'm sorry."

She looked at him. "I wonder if you are."

"Do you doubt me?" There was no bitterness in his voice—he wanted to know.

"What I think doesn't matter. Eliot, I can't work for you. It wouldn't be proper. You're entitled to your fresh start, but I can't be a part of it. I wish you well." Their drinks arrived. She didn't touch hers. "If you want me to leave now I will."

"No—no, don't leave. I've changed in so many ways thanks to you." He raised his glass of scotch to her, as if in a toast. "I owe you, Rowena Willow."

THEY FINISHED dinner early. It wasn't so much unfriendly as awkward, their relationship finally, Rowena felt, coming to an end. Eliot Tyhurst promised to keep in touch. She assured him she was glad he had paid her a visit upon his release from prison and once again wished him well.

She grabbed a taxi outside the hotel and asked the driver to take her to Sofia Scarlatti's apartment a block from Mario's Bar & Grill on the waterfront. She had looked up the address in her telephone book and, of course, remembered it.

Sometimes she wondered if she remembered too damned much.

A sudden fog had descended over the city. Rowena shut her eyes and breathed in its dampness. It wasn't even nine o'clock; Joe's widowed grandmother might still be up. Rowena would make up her mind whether to bother her when she got there.

"Here you go," the driver said.

She paid him and climbed out onto the curb. So close to the water, the fog was thicker, enveloping her in its silence. She went up the short walk to the main entrance of the three-story stucco building. About a half-dozen rosebushes were tangled together on a wooden fence, their riot of color penetrating the gray fog.

Rowena hesitated at the front door. There was a light on inside, but she didn't know if Sofia Scarlatti had the first-floor apartment. The upper two floors were dark. Would she only frighten the old woman, banging on her door uninvited?

"Go on up," Joe Scarlatti said behind her.

She spun around in surprise, stopped just short of screaming. She could tell nothing from his expression, whether he was angry at having her there, shocked, saddened. Her own expression, she was sure, betrayed her uncontrolled reaction to his overpowering sensuality. Every fiber of her being wanted to touch him again, to feel him inside her again and again.

It was madness.

He said matter-of-factly, "My grandmother's a night owl."

"Did you follow me?"

"Yep."

"All along? I mean, you followed me to the hotel, then here?"

"Right again."

"But I . . ." She remembered her anger and straightened her shoulders. "Never mind."

Joe grinned. "You were going to say you never saw me, weren't you? I'm pretty good at what I do once I know what I'm up against." His gaze darkened. "And I wasn't going to leave you to Tyhurst no matter how mad you were at me."

"Are, Scarlatti. I'm still mad."

He moved toward her. "No you're not."

She wasn't. She knew she wasn't. "I want to be."

"Yeah. That I can understand." An outside light came on. Joe grinned. "Uh-oh, Granny's on the prowl. She doesn't miss a trick. You go on in. I'll wait out here." He trotted up the steps as a tiny elderly woman pulled open the door. "Grandma," he said lovingly, giving her a kiss on the cheek and a quick hug. "Somebody here to see you, a friend of mine."

Sofia Scarlatti answered him in Italian. He answered her back. Then she shoved him aside and gave Rowena a wide, friendly smile. "Come in, come in, don't stand out there in the rain." Her smile broadened. "We'll let Joe do that!"

He shot Rowena a look that she realized was a warning not to point out to her grandmother that it wasn't raining. One, she could see, did not contradict Sofia Scarlatti.

Joe settled down on the top step, just under an overhang.

Rowena went inside.

"My, my, you're all dressed up," the old woman said, eyeing her guest's flowing, expensive dress as she led her down a short, narrow hall.

"I've been out to dinner—"

"Not with Joe," she said. It wasn't a question.

"No, I—"

"I'd skin him alive if he went out wearing those holey jeans with a pretty woman. I don't know how often I've told him I'd mend them." Like her grandson, Sofia Scarlatti, Rowena noticed, didn't have a trace of an Italian accent, yet she spoke the language of her ancestors fluently. "Come in, sit down. Would you like a nice glass of brandy?"

"That would be lovely, yes. Mrs. Scarlatti, my name is Rowena Willow—"

"I know. Joe told me, but he didn't need to. I'd have remembered you from the trial."

"Eliot Tyhurst's trial," Rowena said unnecessarily.

"Yes."

There was a note of finality to Mrs. Scarlatti's tone, as if they were talking about something very much over and done with. Already Rowena could see that Sofia Scarlatti was not a woman who dwelled in the past; she lived in the present. They went into a brightly lit, simple kitchen, much in need of remodeling, and she seated her guest at a small table covered with an attractive, if worn, cloth splashed with grapevines.

In the light, Rowena guessed that Joe's grandmother was closer to eighty than seventy and not over five feet tall, her hair snow white, her face heavily lined. But her movements and smile were quick, and her dark eyes— her grandson's eyes—missed nothing.

She filled two glasses with brandy and set them on the table. "I wished I'd never heard of Eliot Tyhurst," she said, sitting down. "We were too complacent, my Mario and I. We believed a man like that wouldn't rob two old people. And he didn't. He robbed hundreds of old people!"

"He abused your trust in him. It could happen to anyone."

"To you?"

Rowena shrugged, remembering Joe's earlier words. "We all have financial setbacks, even catastrophes. We try to know the risks but we can't always. That's what was so terrible about what Tyhurst did—he didn't give you the information you needed to make your decision. He didn't inform you of the true risks."

"We didn't ask enough questions."

"Buyer beware? That doesn't always save you from deceit. Tyhurst was an expert. You're no more at fault than if you'd been robbed on the street at gunpoint."

Sofia Scarlatti wrinkled her nose. "I'd have been at fault if I'd been stupid enough to carry everything I own in my pockets! Ten, twenty dollars, you let it go—but everything? No, that's my fault." Her tone was matter-of-fact. She seemed more embarrassed by her ordeal than embittered.

"I really do think you're being hard on yourself, Mrs. Scarlatti," Rowena said. She tried her brandy; it was strong but smooth, and more welcome than she wanted to admit. She pushed aside an image of Joe on his grandmother's front stoop. "I'm very good with this sort of thing and it took me a long time to unravel Tyhurst's scheme. If someone put a little grass or dirt in your lasagna you'd know it, wouldn't you?"

"I should think so," Sofia Scarlatti said.

"But what if they mashed the grass so thoroughly you couldn't detect it? What if they carefully mixed the dirt with the meat? You might know something's wrong but you might not figure it out right away. Someone who doesn't know lasagna might not even realize anything was wrong. Is that their fault?"

"You're saying you know money. I know lasagna."

"I'm saying we all have our areas of expertise and that Eliot Tyhurst deliberately used his against the very people who put their trust in him. It would be like you putting ingredients you know are bad into your lasagna and then feeding it to your own children."

Mrs. Scarlatti leaned back in her chair and regarded Rowena thoughtfully. "I see your point. I can tell you, though, I'd never make the same mistake with the likes of Eliot Tyhurst again. But I won't get that chance. I have no money left to invest."

"Others learned from your 'mistake.' It won't be so easy for the Eliot Tyhursts of the world to get away with such larceny in the future."

"I suppose it's something, serving as an example," Sofia Scarlatti said, a surprising twinkle in her alert eyes, "but I'd rather have my money!"

Rowena smiled. "I'm sure you would."

"My Joe, he thinks his grandfather died a broken man, but I want you to know he didn't. He died of a heart attack. He'd had a bad heart for years. He was angry with himself, yes, for trusting Tyhurst, but he'd survived much worse hardships in his life than losing his money." She sipped her brandy, studying Rowena. "You know, my Joe needs a good woman in his life."

"I can't cook lasagna."

"Who cares? You know money."

JOE REALIZED he was probably going to go through life being periodically mystified by Rowena Willow.

All she said upon leaving his grandmother's apartment was, "I found the grass, but I haven't even looked for the dirt."

He didn't bother trying to figure that one out.

He got her into the car he'd borrowed from a friend for the express purpose of tracking her. It was one she hadn't seen before and therefore her computer-mind wouldn't remember.

She didn't even comment on it. She just climbed into the front seat and stared straight ahead.

Joe started the engine and glanced sideways at her. Strands of hair had come out of her twist and fallen down her forehead and the back of her neck. Very sexy. Most of her lipstick had come off during dinner, and she'd never bothered to apply a fresh coat. Even sexier. And her dress—

But the woman was thinking about grass and dirt.

"How'd your dinner with Tyhurst go?" he asked.

Nothing. Just that glassy-eyed stare out the window.

"My grandmother liked you. I could tell because she gave you the good brandy. She's got some rotgut you wouldn't believe. Keeps it around for the landlord." She'd been carrying her glass when she saw Rowena to the door and thrust a helping of some leftovers wrapped in aluminum foil at Joe. He could never leave empty-handed, even if he hadn't actually gone inside for a visit. "I don't know what's in the foil but it's probably good. Granny's a hell of a cook. She does great Italian, of course, but also Mexican. Makes a terrific dish she created, sort of a taco lasagna."

He was talking to himself. He knew it. Rowena's mind was occupied in some realm he couldn't access.

Back on Telegraph Hill, he had to hunt for a parking place. If Hank Ryan hadn't told him about the prison-mate who claimed Eliot Tyhurst was a cold-blooded bastard out for revenge, Joe might have let Rowena off at her front door. As it was, he didn't plan to let her out of his sight.

Not that she noticed.

Joe pulled into a tight parking space, turned off the engine and unlocked his door.

Rowena just sat there.

"We're here," he said.

She might have been catatonic.

He touched her shoulder. "Rowena."

She screamed and jerked up, looking as if he'd jumped her in a dark alley. More hair escaped from its pins. Catching her breath, she looked around at him, her eyes wide and faraway. "I'm sorry, I'm thinking . . ."

And she was out of the car and on her way, turning right when she needed to turn left even though this was her own neighborhood. She might as well have been on the damned moon for all she was aware of her sur-roundings. Joe caught up with her and took her by the shoulders and pointed her in the right direction. Not only did she not look embarrassed, she didn't even look *aware* he'd touched her.

Unlike last night, he thought.

"Eccentric geniuses," he muttered. "Who can figure?"

He fell in behind her, observing as she unlocked her door and pushed it open and dropped her purse and turned on lights and headed upstairs, on automatic pilot. She was oblivious to what was around her, lost in her world of thought.

Joe assumed he was in for a long night and headed back to the kitchen to find the cats, Mega and Byte. Hell of a couple of names for two not-so-bad cats. He liked them because they could play fetch, almost like dogs except they had sharper claws.

"Hey, kitties," he said when they didn't pad out to greet him. "Mega? Byte?"

He called them a few more times, whistling and clapping his hands, but they didn't show up. He checked their dishes. Rowena, still in full snit, had fed them before she'd left for her dinner with Eliot Tyhurst.

The cats had hardly touched a bite.

Joe's cop instincts kicked into gear. Every part of him went on high alert. He stopped calling the cats. He backed up toward the kitchen wall and listened.

Something was wrong.

Then he heard a scratching at the pantry door. He opened it, and Mega and Byte wandered out. They were genius's cats, he knew, but cats, he didn't care how smart, couldn't close themselves up in pantries like that.

And then he heard Rowena scream.

"DON'T SCREAM," Eliot Tyhurst said.

Rowena stepped backward toward her computer desk, trying to control her terror. "You startled me."

"You were so intent on destroying me, you just didn't hear me." He nodded at her blank monitor. "Find anything?"

She licked her lips. Her heart was beating much too fast. He had interrupted her high level of concentration, scared the proverbial living daylights out of her. He must have used the key Joe had warned her not to keep outside to get into her house. He must have hidden while she and Joe were at his grandmother's.

Although she'd gotten over his startling her, her heart rate hadn't diminished, and her fear had only grown. She felt nothing but dread.

Eliot Tyhurst, she thought, hadn't reformed. Joe was right.

"You know what I found," she told him. "The dirt in the lasagna—a personal account, very well hidden, containing a half-million dollars you neglected to mention to the authorities was yours. You're not broke, Eliot. You never were."

"No." He smiled coldly, taking a step toward her. "I never was."

Any facade of gentlemanly demeanor had vanished. His eyes were blue ice. His hair was standing on end. His shirt was half-untucked, his tie askew. Spittle had collected at the corners of his mouth. There was blood on his lower lip where he must have bit down too hard.

Rowena had never seen anyone so consumed by hatred.

Hatred of *her*. It was very specific, and very vicious.

She wondered if Joe had heard her scream. Wondered if she should hope he had—or hope, for his sake, that he hadn't. She needed to think and get out of this one herself.

"You never wanted to hire me," she said. "You only wanted to make sure I didn't uncover your secret account."

"You're wrong, Rowena." If possible, his eyes became even icier. "You didn't know about that account three years ago. I fooled you then. I thought I could fool you again. What you don't realize is that I have an even greater purpose in contacting you after all this time."

He reached behind him, into the waistband of his elegant suit pants, and withdrew a gun. It was small and silver, and he pointed it at Rowena.

"Even with a half-million dollars, there's no way I can stay in the United States. I have to leave the country." He sounded aggrieved, as if he were the one who had endured the greater wrong, not the people he'd duped. He went on, "It's all planned. Once I knew I'd have to act tonight, I purchased tickets to South America. I'll be out of here for good in another hour." He smiled. "*With* my money."

"Why didn't you just go? Why risk coming here?"

"Revenge, Rowena. You ruined me. You *destroyed* me. I have no family, no friends, no country, no *life* thanks to you. Do you think I could just vanish without repaying you in kind for what you did to me?"

"So you're going to shoot me." She hated how her voice cracked, but she knew she needed to keep him talking, needed to give Joe a chance to act. "Your revenge is to shoot me."

He shook his head sadly, looking hurt. "I could never shoot you, unless, of course, you leave me no other option."

With his free hand, he removed a length of twine from his suit coat pocket and ordered her to cross her wrists at the small of her back and turn around. She did so. She had no choice.

He tied her wrists fast and hard, squeezing off the blood supply to her hands.

"I've dreamed of this moment for three years," he said harshly, his breath hot and foul on the side of her face. "It feels even better than I imagined."

"And you've fallen even further than I'd ever imagined possible. I feel sorry for you, Eliot."

"You arrogant bitch."

He caught her twisted hair into his hand and pulled hard. Tears sprung into her eyes at the pain. He shoved her down onto the floor, and without ceremony, he snatched up her feet, binding them together with another length of twine.

Where the hell was Scarlatti when she needed him?

Tyhurst kicked her in the thigh, pushing her under her desk. "You can die under your damned computer."

Then he was gone.

And in a moment she smelled smoke.

Ignoring the pain in her hands and feet, Rowena inched backward out from under her desk. Smoke was everywhere above her. She could hear the crackle of flames. Smell the gasoline Tyhurst had used to start the fire.

She flipped over onto her bottom and sat up, her nostrils and mouth filling with smoke. She coughed. "Joe!" she yelled.

There was no answer.

"Scarlatti, where are you? The bastard's got a gun!"

Smoke billowed in from the hall where Tyhurst had obviously started the fire. Rowena grasped a filing drawer with her numb fingers and pulled herself to her feet, into the deadly smoke. She kept an artist's knife in her mug of pens and pencils. Coughing, perspiring, she got it out with her mouth and dropped back down to the floor, tucking her knees up under her chin and immediately getting to work on her bound ankles. If she could get free, she could break a window, climb out onto the rickety, ancient fire-escape ladder.

If only Joe Scarlatti had sense enough not to brave an armed man and a fire to get to her. But that was his job.

The smoke was thickening, stinging her eyes, making her work nearly impossible. She didn't stop. She sawed relentlessly at the twine. It was around her ankles in four layers. If she could get through two, surely the other two would be loose enough to permit her to work them free, or at least to walk.

One layer snapped.

She started immediately on the next one. She could no longer see through her tears and could barely hold on to the knife in her mouth with her coughing, but it didn't matter. She had her rhythm down. And she had to get out, find Joe.

Don't let Tyhurst be his undoing. Please don't let it, if not for my sake, for his grandmother's sake . . .

Somewhere from beyond the flames she heard a shot. "No!"

The second layer snapped.

With a sudden burst of energy, she forced her ankles apart, oblivious to the pain of the twine bearing into her skin.

She was free.

"Joe," she yelled, "I'm all right. I'll go out the fire escape!"

How, she thought, with her hands still bound?

She had to find a way. She had to!

Then his voice came to her over the roar of the flames that were consuming Aunt Adelaide's house. "Rowena!"

And he was there, coming through the flames and the smoke, hair and clothes singed, smoldering. Blood poured down his arm. Rowena stumbled toward him. Her feet ached as circulation returned and blood rushed through them.

"Rowena," he said again, "thank God."

"Tyhurst?"

"Threw him off the second-floor landing. Probably didn't kill him. We gotta get out of here."

"I know, there's a fire escape, if you can manage to cut my hands free—"

She stopped, and time seemed suspended. Something was terribly wrong about the way he was looking at her. "Joe?"

"You'll have to give me a knife or a pair of scissors and I'll get you free. Come on, hurry."

"Joe—"

His face was filled with grime and pain. He blinked, and she knew.

He touched her arm. "It's okay, love, but I can't see."

12

ROWENA PACED outside Joe's hospital room.

It was late, after midnight. Hank Ryan had come, Sofia Scarlatti, Mario. Joe was holding his own, the doctors had said. The bullet had only skimmed his left upper arm. The effect on him of smoke inhalation wasn't as severe as they'd first anticipated. His burns were all first-degree.

But he still couldn't see. Smoke, a blow to the head, heat—even the doctors weren't yet sure what had caused his blindness.

Hank put a big hand on her shoulder. "You sure you don't want to have a doctor look at you? Place is crawling with them."

"No, I'm fine." Even to herself her voice sounded faraway. She rubbed her raw wrists. Blinded and bleeding, Joe had managed to cut her free. And she had managed to get him down the fire escape. "I'll just be coughing up smoke and stuff for a few days."

Hank nodded. She had given him her statement. She didn't know what Joe had told him. A neighbor had called the police and the fire department. Eliot Tyhurst was in custody, being treated not too far from Joe Scarlatti for, as Hank had put it, the thrashing of his life. He would be charged with attempted murder.

The fire department had put out the fire on the third floor of Cedric Willow's strange house before it had spread to any of the other floors. She'd rescued her cats. A neighbor had offered to take them in.

"Do you have a place to stay?" Hank asked.

"I haven't thought that far ahead."

"My wife and I would be happy to have you."

"I'll keep that in mind. Thank you."

He sighed, dropping his hand from her shoulder. "I'm getting you a cup of strong coffee. You need it."

"But I don't drink coffee."

"How could you be in love with Joe Scarlatti and not drink coffee?" He managed a soft laugh, laced with concern for his wounded friend. "I always told him the woman who'd get him would surprise the hell out of everyone, including him. You break the molds, Rowena Willow. Give me five minutes. If I can find you tea, I'll do it. Otherwise it's coffee."

She made herself meet his eyes. They were so dark, so filled with pain for a fellow policeman, a friend. "Thank you."

"Yeah."

A moment later Sofia Scarlatti joined her. "He'll be fine, my Joe. I've seen him in lots worse shape."

"What about his sight?" Rowena asked softly.

She patted Rowena's hand. "We'll just have to wait and see."

Hank returned with a cup of coffee that tasted surprisingly good to Rowena. "You ready to head out?" he asked.

She shook her head. "I'd like to see Joe one more time."

"I'll be out here."

The doctors and nurses had retreated for the time being, and Joe was dozing in his dimly lit room. Rowena leaned over him and realized she was crying only when she saw her tears glistening on his cheek. His eyes were bandaged, his wounded arm, his burns treated. He wasn't in danger of dying. He *would* recover.

But would he see again?

He stirred, and found her hand, squeezed it gently. "You still here?"

"Always."

"I smell coffee. Someone with you?"

"No, it's mine. Hank brought me a cup."

"Life is full of surprises," he said, startling her with his undampered humor.

"I don't know, it tastes all right to me, not that I'd know the difference. Maybe the smoke killed my taste buds."

"You're okay?"

"I'm fine. You?"

He stroked the top of her hand with his thumb. "Go on and get some rest, Rowena. You don't need to stick around."

"I can't leave. Joe, I owe you so much—"

"You don't owe me anything," he said sharply, cutting her off. He dropped her hand. "I was just doing my job."

Her one consolation was that he couldn't see the hurt that washed over her. But she knew what he was doing. He was pushing her away because he was injured, blinded, and his future was uncertain. He didn't want to burden her.

It wasn't going to work.

SHE ENDED UP staying in Joe's apartment above Mario's Bar & Grill because his cousin insisted it was what Joe would want if he were in any frame of mind to articulate what he wanted. As it was, Joe said he thought Rowena should stay with a friend or get a room at a hotel, charge her insurance company.

"Ignore him," was Mario's advice.

Hank Ryan and his wife had her over for dinner. Sofia Scarlatti loaded up the refrigerator and cupboards and checked her grandson's apartment for "vermin," pronouncing it habitable after a close inspection. Mario prepared her low-fat eggplant parmesan and low-fat bean chili and bought a case of mineral water to keep on hand.

Her life was changing, had changed, and although so much of that change was out of her control, Rowena was surprised and delighted. And amazed at how good it felt to rely on other people, not just herself.

Her own friends came to her assistance without prodding and provided her with technical and personal support in salvaging, repairing and restoring her office, damaged by smoke and water. The fire itself hadn't got that far. She would be back in business soon.

But where? And under what circumstances?

Right now, however, for once, she wasn't preoccupied with the future.

She spent as much time as she could every day with Joe, staying until he or the doctors kicked her out. He was clearly trying to keep his distance. She didn't press, but they found themselves talking about their lives, their hopes, their regrets. They exchanged funny stories, and some sad ones.

They became friends.

Away from the hospital, Rowena discovered that Joe Scarlatti led a life filled with people. She enjoyed the coziness of his apartment, the constant presence of family, friends, perfect strangers. She got to know his neighborhood. And she realized that she couldn't go back to her old life, to its relative isolation. Instead, she found that she wanted things she'd long thought she was too different, too odd, to have—a little house, a garden, a yard. She wanted to give parties.

She wanted to have children.

She wanted to have a husband.

Joe Scarlatti had changed her perspective on her life and her future. Loving him had changed *her*.

On a cool, bright morning a week after their ordeal with Eliot Tyhurst, she was nursing a pot of tea and going over a report for a client at what she'd come to know as Joe's booth at Mario's Bar & Grill.

Mario burst out of the kitchen. "The hospital just called. Joe's getting sprung today, Row." He always called her Row now. "He can see."

JOE GRINNED when Rowena came into his room. "Aren't you a sight for sore eyes."

He meant it. He had never seen her look so alive and beautiful. After two weeks of darkness, he drank in the sight of her. Her eyes were as blue as the California sky. Her gleaming spun-gold hair hung down her back in a thick French braid. And she had on jeans. Rowena Willow in jeans. It was a sight to see.

He couldn't stop smiling.

"I've come to take you home," she said, and tears sprang into her eyes. "I'm so glad, Joe...I couldn't...if I'd been responsible for your losing your sight..."

He touched her cheek, gently brushed away a tear with his knuckle. "You wouldn't have been responsible."

She held her breath. "I never thought I'd hear those words from you, Joe Scarlatti."

"I know it. I've had a lot of time to think these past few days in a way I haven't let myself think in months. You weren't responsible for what happened to me any more—" for a moment, he choked on his words "—any more than I was responsible for Matt's death. I miss the crazy bastard—I guess I always will. But it wasn't my fault."

Rowena smiled through her tears and kissed him about a quarter-inch from his right eye. "You look terrific."

Desire shot through him, hot and electric. If she'd kissed him on the mouth, he'd have hauled her down onto his hospital bed and made love to her. As it was, it was all he could do to finish buttoning his shirt. He already had on his jeans. All he had to do now was put on his sneakers and be gone.

"So," he said, "are we taking a bus back?"

"Nope."

"You're driving?"

"Uh-huh. You're in for a surprise, Sergeant Scarlatti."

He suspected this wouldn't be an uncommon event. But he was sure about one important thing—how he felt about her. "You don't own a car."

"I've got your truck." And she reached into her jeans pocket and withdrew his keys, dangling them in front of him.

"You're going to drive my truck—"

She grinned at him. "I've *been* driving it."

"Mario gave you the keys?"

She nodded without a hint of guilt. Her eyes were sparkling the way Joe had imagined them for the past week.

"What else haven't you told me?" he asked.

"Well, your grandmother has started to teach me how to knit and crochet and says she's going to teach me how to make lasagna, but I don't know—she puts sausage in her lasagna. And Mario taught me how to pour beer. I helped Hank and his wife put up a new swing set for his kids—you should see the thing, it's even got a tent." She licked her lips. "And I've been staying at your apartment."

He just stared at her. She seemed very pleased with herself. Smug, even. Like she'd outwitted him just as she had that very first day when she'd spotted him out on her street. It seemed so damned long ago. What had his life been like before Rowena Willow came into it?

"My apartment," he repeated.

"Yep. I'd have told you except I thought picturing me sleeping alone in your bed might inhibit your recovery."

She was out of the room and into the corridor before he could grab her.

"By the way," she told him on their way out to the parking lot, "I had the oil in your truck changed. It needed it."

"You *had* it changed?"

She glanced sideways at him. "I don't do oil, Sergeant."

"I'll remember that."

"I did vacuum and clean the interior. I found an old doughnut under the seat. I called the Smithsonian to see if they were interested—"

"Very funny. I hope you didn't touch any of my guns."

She shook her head. "Guns make me nervous."

She fell silent and Joe reached out to touch her arm.

"I was scared," she said suddenly, in a quiet voice. "When Tyhurst pulled out that gun and tied me up . . ."

"Should you have been anything else but scared?"

"I don't know. Sometimes I think I was pretty cowardly, complying with him the way I did."

"Rowena, if you hadn't done as he asked, he would have shot you."

They headed out into the bright day, and Joe inhaled the cool air, relishing his freedom. The doctors had given his eyes a clean bill of health. Told him to take it easy for a few days.

"Were you scared?" she asked as they crossed the parking lot.

"Yeah. Scared and madder than hell. I thought the bastard had killed you." He hesitated, then decided he might as well tell her the rest of it. "I didn't care what happened to me. I saw those cats and knew he was there, then heard you scream—it was all I could do not to barrel up the stairs and have at him. But I kept my cool."

"Your training took over," Rowena said. "Your instincts. You trusted yourself."

He shrugged. "I wasn't thinking about that. I was just thinking about wringing Tyhurst's neck. He figured he'd be as good with a gun as he is with a con, but he wasn't. I took him by surprise—or at least enough by surprise that he only got off that one shot." Joe's eyes darkened suddenly. "I had him hanging over the stairs, Rowena. I could have flipped him over the side, killed him."

"You're not an Eliot Tyhurst," Rowena said.

"No, I'm not." He shook off his gloom and grinned at her. "A cop 'til the bitter end, Rowena. That's what I am."

His truck was cleaner than he'd seen it in months, and impeccably parked between two white lines. "What'd you do, get out a ruler and *measure?*"

"Parking crooked is so discourteous in tight quarters like this."

Discourteous? Joe climbed in the front seat and waited while she climbed in behind the wheel, her long braid flopped down her front. "You do that when you're self-conscious, you know—talk in that prim way. I've had a week just of listening to you, without the distraction of seeing you. I've noticed."

She scowled. "I am who I am."

"Yeah. You are. It's been fun to figure out just who you are."

"And you have that figured out?"

"Working on it."

She used more gas than he would have to start the engine. He went to warn her about how fickle reverse could be, but she seemed to know already and jammed the gearshift down hard, so it wouldn't jump out, just as he would have. He watched her maneuver the finicky old truck out of the parking space and out to the street.

"Not bad," he said.

"It can be exasperating on the hills. I almost rolled into a car a few times when I had to keep stopping and going. An automatic transmission is definitely easier in San Francisco, in my opinion. Have you ever considered trading this thing in?"

"No."

She smiled. "You didn't even hesitate. Well, I've found I enjoy driving. I might have to invest in my own car."

On that first day when he'd rung her doorbell, Joe would have asked her why someone who didn't go anywhere needed a car. But in their long talks over the past week, he had heard in her a pent-up longing to go, to do, to see. Rowena Willow had a zest for adventure he'd never have guessed possible when he'd watched her arrive in her tower sunroom just after five every afternoon.

He noticed she wasn't taking the most direct route back to Mario's Bar & Grill. Maybe she didn't know it. "Rowena, where are we going?"

"Telegraph Hill," she said.

"Why?"

"I want—I need to show you something."

When they came to her quiet, exclusive street, Joe saw nothing unusual, nothing changed. The fire damage was restricted to the interior. From the outside, Rowena Willow's little castle looked as weird as ever.

Except there *was* a group of people milling about outside. About a half-dozen. They were well dressed, gesturing and talking excitedly.

"Looks like a committee meeting," Joe said.

"It is. Before I tell you about it, however, I need to get a few things straight with you."

"Okay."

She'd double-parked in front of her house. Joe didn't point out that that was more "discourteous" than being a little crooked within a parking space.

"First of all," she said, still gripping the wheel with both hands, "you weren't just 'doing your job' last week with Tyhurst. If you will recall, you weren't on duty. You were—and are—still on leave of absence from the department. Our association was unofficial."

She glanced at him, apparently to see if he had any comment, and he said, "Are those my jeans you're wearing?"

He almost got a smile. "You're impossible, you know that? I'm trying to have a serious conversation. Will you allow that you weren't just doing your job?"

"I'm a cop, Rowena. It's who I am."

"Yes, I know that." She pursed her lips. "But you don't—um—make love to all the citizens of San Francisco, do you?"

A corner of his mouth twitched. "Not all."

She sighed, exercising supreme patience. "You stayed in my house with me. After you were hurt, I stayed at your apartment."

"Without my knowledge," he observed. "You know, I think those *are* my jeans."

This time she just ignored him. "Your family and friends took me under their wing. I've visited you every day. I've been driving your truck all around town." She looked over at him, her eyes huge and luminous. "I'm wearing your jeans."

"Dammit, I knew they were mine!"

"I think I have longer legs than you do."

Joe didn't know why he didn't just drag her out of the truck and cart her upstairs to one of Aunt Adelaide's strange rooms.

"And I certainly have a smaller waist," she said.

Hell, he'd even make love to her in with the critters.

"My point is," she went on crisply, "that you can't just push me out of your life when bad things happen."

Joe grew serious. "Rowena, falling for a man like me is dangerous."

"I'm not falling for a man like you. I'm falling for *you*. Have fallen, I should say. Your profession carries with it certain risks. I accept that. Life's a risky business. And retreating from it doesn't lessen the risks. I was just sitting in my office minding my own business when something about Eliot Tyhurst's financial activities caught my eye. Look how dangerous that proved to be."

Joe digested her words, raking a hand through his hair and staring out at the people on the sidewalk. One was pointing to Rowena's tower room. "Tell me about the committee," he said.

She hesitated. He knew that what she'd just told him, how she'd just exposed herself, hadn't been easy for her. He understood, even if he hadn't yet acknowledged it to her.

"They're from the historical society. I contacted them a few days ago. It turns out they've had their eye on the Willow house for a long time—I had no idea. When I told them that Aunt Adelaide had made very few changes from Cedric's day, and I very few changes from her day, they were ecstatic."

Joe turned in time to see her run her tongue along the bottom of her lip, then bite down with her top teeth. She still had the steering wheel in her grip.

She went on, "But when I told them I would consider donating the house and its entire contents to them, they were speechless."

"So am I," Joe said.

She smiled at him. "You're never speechless, Sergeant Scarlatti."

"It's a valuable piece of property. The fire damage was confined to the third floor. You'd be giving up a fortune."

"I make a good living doing what I do," she said. "And I want to be free. I want my own house, my own furnishings, my own garden."

"You won't keep anything?"

"Just a few personal things Aunt Adelaide gave me, and any Willow family pictures and papers. Not Cedric's portrait, though." She nodded to the house her great-grandfather had built. "It belongs here."

"I see," Joe said.

"I just wanted you to know."

She pried one hand loose from the wheel, turned the key in the ignition and started back down Telegraph Hill.

For a long time Joe didn't say anything. He had to process what Rowena had just done.

Finally, he said, "You're not even keeping one dead bird?"

"Not one."

"Good. I did kind of like the owl in the library, but I'd probably get the heebie-jeebies having a beady-eyed thing like that hanging around my place."

"*Your* place?"

"Our place, then."

"Scarlatti—"

"There is one thing I'm going to arm-wrestle the historical society for, though—Sir Lancelot in the front hall. I figure the only way I'm going to be a valiant prince is to have a suit of armor kicking around for the right occasion."

"Aunt Adelaide purchased it." She was going along with him, he could tell, showing him she understood what he was trying to say. "I suppose I could speak to the committee."

"I figure it can be payment for my having saved your ass."

"Mine! I saved yours! You'd have been burned alive if I hadn't got you down that fire escape."

"Naw, I'd have found my way out. You, on the other hand, would never have gotten out of there if I hadn't freed your wrists."

"No way. If you'd have managed blind, I'd have managed bound."

"You're stubborn, Rowena," he said, enjoying himself, "and you're wrong."

"I'm not wrong."

He grinned at her. "Quite the shrinking violet, aren't you? Well, I warn you, I'm not one to back down from a good fight. I'm not easy to live with."

"Neither am I," she said.

"Oh, I already know that."

"You'll always be this honest?"

"Always."

"We're not a disaster together, Joe, are we?"

"Depends on your point of view, I guess. From mine, no, we're far, far from a disaster together. What about yours?"

She smiled. "No."

He sat back. "Great. Now, do I get the armor?"

Epilogue

JOE GOT the armor.

The historical society considered it a small price to pay for a valuable historic house on Telegraph Hill, built by one of San Francisco's true rich eccentrics. He tried setting it up in Mario's, but his cousin came after him with a carving knife and Joe carted it upstairs to his apartment.

Rowena had been out looking at office space in a real office building. When she came back, she found Joe kneeling over the damned thing. "It won't fit in here standing upright," he said, not looking at her. "Ceilings are too low. Guess we're going to have to get busy finding a place of our own."

"Your grandmother will be thrilled. She's been clipping ads."

Finally, he looked at her. And his jaw, literally, dropped. She realized he was as close to speechless as he probably would ever get. "Rowena," he managed to say.

She ran both hands through her hair, still getting used to its new length. "I stopped by a hair salon on impulse. Do you know, I'd never been to one? It was quite an experience. I thought they were going to throw me out because I didn't have an appointment, but—"

"But once they saw your hair, they couldn't let you out of there."

"I told them to take off a good eighteen inches."

Joe climbed to his feet, never taking his eyes from her.

She liked the feel of her freshly cut hair. It was still long—below her shoulders—but she relished its bounce, its lightness. She felt free.

He was in front of her now, touching it. "It's beautiful."

She smiled. "I might never wear it up again."

ONLY DAYS LATER—when they had a house all picked out and Mario already had a couple hundred meatballs in the freezer for their wedding—did Joe discover the little surprise Rowena had in store for him when he was sorting through a bunch of junk in his bedroom closet.

He damned well almost screamed. Him, a tough cop. He'd returned to the force a week ago, ending his self-imposed leave of absence. It felt good to be back. Still, who the hell wouldn't be shocked by a pair of beady eyes staring from inside a dark closet?

"Rowena!"

She materialized behind him. "Oh, I see you've found Arnold."

"Arnold? It's a goddamned dead bird!"

"It was my great-grandfather's favorite."

Joe stepped back so the overhead light could angle in and he could see better. Yep, it was the stuffed owl from the library. He looked around at Rowena, all gorgeous from her haircut, as free and loose as he had ever imagined her. His heart seemed ready to burst with loving her. How had he survived those horrible six months on leave, before he'd met her? He didn't think he'd ever felt this alive.

And something became clear to him now, with the damned stuffed owl staring down at him, that hadn't been clear before.

"You know something, Ms. Willow?"

"I know a lot of things, Sergeant Scarlatti."

"Yeah, you're an eccentric genius. You know a hell of a lot of things. Did you know that you didn't rescue me?"

"Yes, I did."

He shook his head. "Nope." He wrapped her in his arms and pulled her close. "We rescued each other."

A Note from Carla Neggers

When I was a little girl, we lived in a very old house in the country, and among its many "treasures" was a thick, musty, moldy book of fairy tales. I would read them high up in a tree or on a rock in the middle of a brook or upstairs in my bed while listening to the pitter-patter of rain on the roof. They fired my imagination about love and romance, good and evil, honor and betrayal, jealousy and devotion. They opened my mind to human emotions, ideals, strengths and weaknesses on a grand scale.

These days, my idea of romance doesn't involve castles and frogs and white horses, although I still love that stuff. I'm more interested in two whole, independent people who help each other discover, and become more fully, who they are. That's why I chose the story of Rapunzel as inspiration for *Night Watch*. Through their love for each other, Rowena and Joe learn to "let down their hair" in a metaphorical sense, and in the best sense, by freeing their best selves.

Take 4 bestselling love stories FREE

Plus get a FREE surprise gift!

Special Limited-time Offer

Mail to Harlequin Reader Service®

3010 Walden Avenue
P.O. Box 1867
Buffalo, N.Y. 14269-1867

YES! Please send me 4 free Harlequin Temptation® novels and my free surprise gift. Then send me 4 brand-new novels every month, which I will receive before they appear in bookstores. Bill me at the low price of $2.44 each plus 25¢ delivery and applicable sales tax, if any.* That's the complete price and—compared to the cover prices of $2.99 each—quite a bargain! I understand that accepting the books and gift places me under no obligation ever to buy any books. I can always return a shipment and cancel at any time. Even if I never buy another book from Harlequin, the 4 free books and the surprise gift are mine to keep forever.

142 BPA AJHR

Name	(PLEASE PRINT)	
Address		Apt. No.
City	State	Zip

This offer is limited to one order per household and not valid to present Harlequin Temptation® subscriber
*Terms and prices are subject to change without notice. Sales tax applicable in N.Y.

UTEMP-93R   ©1990 Harlequin Enterprises Limited

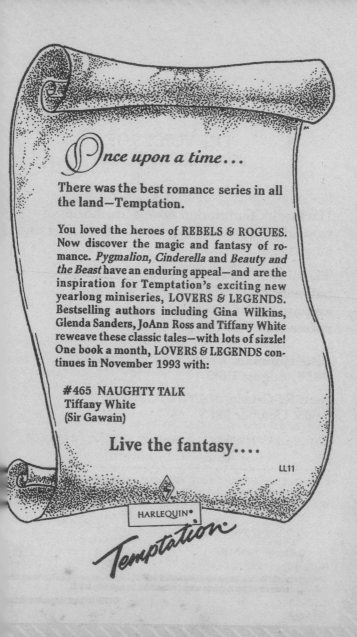

HARLEQUIN®

Temptation®

NEW AUTHOR

THE VOICES OF
TOMORROW TODAY

Sensuous, bold, sometimes controversial, Harlequin Temptation novels are stories of women today—the attitudes, desires, lives and language of the nineties.

The distinctive voices of our authors is the hallmark of Temptation. We are proud to announce two new voices are joining the spectacular Temptation lineup.

Kate Hoffman, *INDECENT EXPOSURE*, #456, August 1993

Jennifer Crusie, *MANHUNTING*, #463, October 1993

Tune in to the hottest station on the romance dial—Temptation!

HARLEQUIN®
Temptation®

FIRST-PERSON PERSONAL

Nothing is more intimate than first-person personal narration....

Two emotionally intense, intimate romances told in first person, in the tradition of Daphne du Maurier's *Rebecca* from bestselling author Janice Kaiser.

Recently widowed Allison Stephens travels to her husband's home to discover the truth about his death and finds herself caught up in a web of family secrets and betrayals. Even more dangerous is the passion ignited in her by the man her husband hated most—Dirk Granville.
BETRAYAL, Temptation #462, October 1993

P.I. Darcy Hunter is drawn into the life of Kyle Weston, the man who had been engaged to her deceased sister. Seeing him again sparks long-buried feelings of love and guilt. Working closely together on a case, their attraction escalates. But Darcy fears it is memories of her sister that Kyle is falling in love with.
DECEPTIONS, Temptation #466, November 1993

Each book tells you the heroine's compelling story in her own personal voice. Wherever Harlequin books are sold.

HTFPP

$\mathcal{O}$*nce upon a time...*

THERE WAS A FABULOUS
PROOF-OF-PURCHASE OFFER
AVAILABLE FROM

HARLEQUIN®

Temptation

As you enjoy your Harlequin Temptation LOVERS & LEGENDS stories each and every month during 1993, you can collect four proofs of purchase to redeem a lovely opal pendant! The classic look of opals is always in style, and this necklace is a perfect complement to any outfit!

One proof of purchase can be found in the back pages of each LOVERS & LEGENDS title ... one every month during 1993!

LIVE THE FANTASY ...

To receive your gift, mail this certificate, along with four (4) proof-of-purchase coupons from any Harlequin Temptation LOVERS & LEGENDS title plus $2.50 for postage and handling (check or money order—do not send cash), payable to Harlequin Books, to: **In the U.S.**: LOVERS & LEGENDS, P.O. Box 9057, Buffalo, NY 14269-9057; **In Canada**: LOVERS & LEGENDS, P.O. Box 622, Fort Erie, Ontario L2A 5X3.

Requests must be received by January 31, 1994.

Allow 4-6 weeks after receipt of order for delivery.

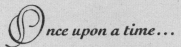

Lovers & Legends

NAME: _____

ADDRESS: _____

_____

CITY: _____

STATE/PROVINCE: _____

ZIP/POSTAL CODE: _____

ONE PROOF OF PURCHASE   084 KAO LLPOPR